Min<

Part One

Books 1-3

Katrina Kahler

Copyright © KC Global Enterprises Pty Ltd

Table of Contents

Book 1

My New Life

The secret...

Have you ever felt that something was meant to be? That perhaps a chance meeting was not so accidental after all; almost as though it had been previously arranged and was waiting to happen.

Being in just the right place at just the right moment has to be more than coincidence. And I am convinced that Millie and I were meant to meet that day. It was as if the opportunity to cross paths had been planned all along. And when Millie accidentally bumped into me in the store, the conversation that followed seemed the most natural thing in the world.

Somehow I had known that our chance meeting would eventuate in a friendship of sorts. Call it intuition or simple gut instinct, but for some reason, I was sure we would hit it off. I also knew that a real friend was something I'd been craving my entire life.

As luck would have it, Millie herself, was in desperate need of a close friend as well. Her best friend, a girl called Julia Jones, had recently moved with her family to the country and Millie was missing her terribly. So for each of us, the timing could not have been better.

Strangely enough, I'd always been able to make friends. For me, that seemed to come easily. The problem lay in keeping them.

New kids at school were always an attraction, and I often found that I had plenty of people interested in becoming my friend and wanting to hang out with me each time I started at a new school. And believe me, this happened a lot!

But the friendships never lasted. Within no time at all, they'd find me weird or strange or creepy; and then do everything they could to avoid me.

So, in time, I learned the secret was to keep my mouth shut. And when we eventually moved to Carindale and I met Millie, I instantly realized it was my opportunity to start over.

"Just don't say anything, Emmie. Keep your comments to yourself!"

They were the words I constantly repeated in my head, ones that my mom had reminded me of on so many occasions but I'd failed to listen to; which of course had resulted in the same consequences each and every time…any and all friendships I'd made were destroyed.

But when it came to Millie. I decided to finally do what I should have been doing all along.

And that was to stay quiet.

There was no way I wanted to jeopardize my chance of finally having a best friend.

That meant never, ever telling her my secret.

I also knew that if I did, my mom would make us move again. And I wanted to avoid that at all costs!

The gift...

Most people probably think that being a mind reader would be amazing. But it's far from it! Take it from one who knows…being able to read minds is definitely not at all what it's made out to be.

Mom called it a "gift." But my so-called "gift" had landed me in trouble on that many occasions, I'd lost count. The worst part was, it seemed to push people away. While it may seem cool to know what other kids are thinking, when they realized that I was constantly picking up on the thoughts in their heads, they quickly found the whole scenario very uncomfortable.

This was because I struggled to keep my reactions to myself and from a young age, I'd constantly blabbed out a comment or a question or an answer even though the other person hadn't spoken. Well, not out loud anyway.

Their looks of surprise were always the same and eventually, they'd avoid me completely. As far as they were concerned, I was creepy. And before I knew it, my status had reverted to "Loner" once again.

Or as I preferred to call it, "Loser" with a capital L.

As time passed, things gradually became worse. My mom's friends started asking questions and acting strangely around us and that was when my mom really started to worry.

"Maybe it's some kind of reaction to the trauma she's experienced," one friend suggested.

"It could be Emmie's way of trying to cope," another helpful friend added.

Then when they insisted I should be checked by a doctor or a psychologist of some sort, Mom decided we had to move, to relocate to a new town where no one knew us.

Within a matter of months, our house was sold and we were on our way, hoping to find a nicer place filled with friendlier and more unsuspecting people. And that had been the beginning of the pattern that followed.

Rather than trying to deal with each situation, my mom's choice was always to run away. And because she owned an online business, she was able to work anywhere that had an Internet connection.

"Let's just leave, Em! The kids at that school aren't nice anyway. We'll move somewhere else. We'll rent a nice new house and you can go to another school where you can make real friends."

Deep down, I knew that she was scared; terrified that someone might learn the truth about her mind-reading daughter. She was convinced if that happened, I'd be in danger of being abducted by some government agency or foreign power, and then I'd be put under lock and key while they conducted ongoing extensive scientific experiments to determine how my brain worked.

It all seemed a bit far-fetched to me, but she was sure that something terrible would happen and she'd never see me again. So, almost daily, she reminded me of the urgent need to stay quiet about what I was capable of doing.

 "You have a gift, Emmie. But it has to be our secret. Ours and ours alone. If anyone finds out, then we will be torn apart. I know it!"

At least my 'lack of friends' problem made relocating easier.

Well, much easier than it would have been if I were a normal, everyday kind of person, I guess; one who didn't have hidden powers that made everyone around her feel uneasy. Although I had to admit, moving house every six to twelve months or so, certainly was over-kill.

This time, however, I was determined to make it work. It was the summer holidays and I had Millie to hang out with.

And in addition to having a real friend, one who did not find me creepy and strange, I also soon discovered that she had some pretty cool friends of her own.

There were a couple of boys in particular who had caught

my eye, and for a change, it seemed that I finally had something to look forward to!

How it all began...

One of my earliest memories is of my 4th birthday. At that time, my dad was still alive and although the memory is vague in parts, it's something I am particularly grateful for because it is one of the few memories I have of my dad.

My mother had made a beautiful cake that she'd covered in decorative flower shapes made from delicious pink icing. It was the prettiest cake I had ever seen.

Sitting excitedly on my dad's lap, I watched Mom light the candles one by one, mesmerized by the sparkling glow in front of me. Then, after waiting patiently for my parents to sing happy birthday, I attempted to blow out each of the four little flames. But they were quite stubborn and continued to remain lit. All the while, the room was filled with happy laughter at my feeble attempts.

It finally took Mom's help and all four flames disappeared. But when I looked into her eyes, instead of the joy that had been there only moments earlier, all I could see was terrible sadness.

"What's wrong with Daddy?" I gasped, turning abruptly towards the face of the man who held me on his lap. "Is he really going to die?"

I'd heard my parents comment before…that I seemed older than my years; that I seemed to know things that I shouldn't, that I was too smart for my own good.
But their reaction in that moment was more of an intense shock than a surprise.

The instant the words had left my lips, the look of horror that appeared on my mother's face, said it all. I'd found out their secret. The one they'd attempted to hide from me, and try as she might to distract me, it was no use. I ran hysterically to my room; the melted blobs of wax sitting in a thick lumpy layer on top of the icing on the cake that I had been in awe of only minutes before.

I remember feeling so scared that I tried to hide in the corner, clutching tightly to the teddy that I had been given at birth and which so many years later, I still kept in a prime position on top of the pillows on my bed.

My father was going to die. I had heard my mother's voice in my head and although I struggled to understand where that voice had come from, I knew what I had heard. And I also knew what death was.

Earlier that year, the puppy my dad had brought home unexpectedly, had been hit by a car and killed. In the short time we had owned that puppy, I'd become so attached that I was heartbroken when he died. And in the process, I learned that death was a permanent thing, causing something or someone you love to disappear and never return. I was terrified that this was going to happen to my father.

My 4th birthday had been the first real sign of my "gift". Sometime later, there was another occasion when once again, I knew exactly what my parents were thinking. I could distinctly hear their voices in my head and it was as though they were speaking directly to me. But when I glanced in their direction, they were sitting at the kitchen table not saying a word.

I replied anyway and I remember my mom laughing and jokingly calling me her little "mind reader".

But rather than being amused, my dad simply frowned and told me I was imagining things.

He hadn't fooled me though. Even at that young age, I knew I had heard their thoughts; the voices were real and not imaginary. And I was also aware that it was not normal to be a "mind reader".

Then, sure enough, it was only a matter of months before my father's illness became obvious and his condition rapidly began to decline. He only lasted another year and then the terminal blood disease that had been making him so ill took his life. After that, my mom and I were left on our own.

I didn't have too many memories of my dad, but I could feel his presence around me. Sometimes it was stronger than others and I knew that he was there. It was a comforting feeling and helped me to cope with all the problems I had to face in the years after he died.

Being constantly labeled as weird, strange or creepy was no fun at all. Sometimes I tried to laugh it off, but deep down inside, it hurt more than anything.

While I attempted to ignore the taunts from the other kids, I could not escape their voices in my head. Even though some were too polite to say the words, "You're a freak" to my face, I knew exactly what they were thinking. I could hear their thoughts as clearly as if they'd spoken them.

And every time Mom and I tried our luck in a new town, the scene was repeated all over again.

Questions...

One Saturday morning, several years after my father's death, I sat alone in my room with my favorite teddy for company and I recalled the day my father passed away. Overwhelmed with sadness at the time, I had taken little notice of the tingling sensation that passed through my body as I held his hand. Sitting at the side of his hospital bed while the machines beeped noisily at his side, I was aware of very little except the faint sound of his breathing.

But for some reason, that morning so many years later, I remembered the strange feeling distinctly. It was kind of a buzzing tingle underneath my skin and it had seemed to work its way into my fingers as my dad took his last breath. The memory became so vivid that I could almost feel that exact sensation once again. It was as though the mysterious power that I'd been gifted with had been transferred in its full intensity from him to me the moment he died.

While there had been a couple of times in my younger years when I'd been able to hear voices in my head, my parents had dismissed my remarks and the situation appeared to be forgotten.

Ever since that tragic day however, I was aware that something unusual was going on and the voices became a much more regular occurrence. It was as if my ability to read minds grew stronger with each passing year. So much so, I eventually had to ask the question that had been worrying me for quite some time.

"Mom, was Dad a mind reader too? Could he read minds like me?"

She looked curiously towards me, a concerned frown appearing on her face as she considered the possibility. I could see that she was tossing the idea around in her head and she was very quiet for a moment, obviously deep in thought over my suggestion.

Her expression gradually changed and I watched carefully as she came to terms with what she had obviously tried to ignore for so long.

Shaking her head in confusion, she replied. "I don't know, Emmie. But if your father could do what you are now capable of, surely I would have known about it. And besides, he confided in me all the time. If he could read minds, don't you think he would have told me?"

She doesn't believe me!

Although Mom tried to deny it, I was convinced that my dad had the "gift" too. I could think of no other explanation. Almost certainly, I must have inherited it from someone. And something deep inside told me that he had been a mind reader as well.

Moving house did nothing for my curiosity though. I still wanted answers. If my dad really was a mind reader, why had he kept it a secret? Why would he not share that detail with Mom? And surely he realized before he died that I'd shown signs of being a mind reader like him.

There were too many questions that I did not know the answers to. I knew there must be an explanation and I was desperate to find it.

Meanwhile, the challenge lay in keeping my secret safe, the way my dad had done. No one could know except Mom and me.

It was up to me to stay quiet and keep all my thoughts and remarks silent. But going by my past record, I wasn't sure if that were possible.

Carindale...

As it turned out, moving to Carindale was the best thing we could have done. We managed to rent a lovely house that was situated only a short distance from the mall; this suited me perfectly because I loved hanging out at the shops and looking for clothes. Ever since my 12th birthday, Mom had given me permission to go to the shops on my own. Not that I was able to buy too much as she only gave me a small allowance. But it was better than always sitting at home on my computer watching YouTube videos or repeats of my favorite television series.

Although my mother worked from home and was usually around, most of the time she was busy working. So she often encouraged me to invite friends over, or at least she attempted to. But whenever I did, the answer was always the same.

"Sorry, I'm busy."

I knew that was a lie though. Their excuses did not fool me. As well as the words they spoke, I also heard the voices in their heads. And I was fully aware of what my 'friends' were really thinking. Sometimes their thoughts were so mean, I'd have to catch my breath.

"OMG! No way!"

"Haha! What a joke! As if I'd give up my weekend to hang out with you."

"You're so weird. There's no way I want to go to your house!"

I would always struggle to prevent the tears that threatened to drip into full view onto my reddened cheeks.

If only I didn't know their true thoughts, at least that way I'd be spared the embarrassment and the humiliation. It was just too upsetting and I could not bear to put myself through it any longer. So in the end, I decided to avoid trying to make friends altogether. It just wasn't worth it.

Until I met Millie that was.

And then, as if by magic, everything changed!

Unexpected excitement…

It was only a few days after Millie and I had first met that I received her text. Being the summer holidays, she was looking for things to do and when she asked if I wanted to hang out at the mall, I could literally feel my excitement bubbling over.

But the moment I replied, I realized I had a problem. Quickly scanning my wardrobe, I searched for something to wear. This was the most important event of my entire life and I couldn't see anything that I was at all interested in changing into. There was no way I could turn up to meet Millie in the old jeans and T-shirt that I'd put on that morning. The situation was a disaster and I could feel a rush of anxiety settling in the pit of my stomach.

I was sure that Millie would be wearing something really nice. Her gorgeous outfit had been the first thing I'd noticed as soon as we bumped into each other. And I was sure that her entire wardrobe was filled with clothes just as pretty.

Thinking back to my mom's invitation to go shopping just the day before, I shook my head in frustration. She'd suggested we go on a bit of a spending spree to celebrate our latest move. But for some stupid reason, I'd decided to postpone the idea until the weekend. Obviously though, if I hadn't made that silly mistake I wouldn't be facing the problem I'd found myself in.

Even though I knew I was to blame, I burst into her office to complain about my lack of clothes. I had to complain to someone and she was always the one forced to deal with my outbursts.

But as soon as I'd finished ranting about how bad my clothing situation was, without a word whatsoever, she turned to her cupboard and pulled out the perfect solution.

In her hands, she held up a very pretty blue and white striped top, one that I'd never seen before but was obviously meant for me. It was almost like a magic act where the magician pulled a rabbit out of a hat and the children gasped with delight. For me, the reaction was exactly the same and I could feel a beaming smile quickly spread across my face. She then explained that she'd bought it as a surprise and when she asked if I'd like to wear it that day, I instantly threw my arms around her neck in a grateful hug.

"Oh Mom, you're a life saver. Thank you so much!! It will go perfectly with my black shorts."

When I looked at my reflection in the bedroom mirror a few minutes later, I was more than happy with the result. I absolutely loved the top and felt so thankful to have been given it.

But then my gaze took in the whole image of the person staring back; big brown eyes, freckles dotted across my nose and cheeks and long brown hair, slightly wavy and in need of a good trim.

I didn't mind my face and hair so much but it was the long skinny legs hanging out the bottom of my shorts that really bothered me. I'd always been tall and lanky, and regardless of the huge amounts of food that I ate, I struggled to put on weight.

"You can eat anything, Emmie. You're so lucky! You could be a fashion model one day."

My mother's words rang in my head when I thought of her amazed reaction each night as she watched me demolish platefuls of food. But her remarks did little to improve my own opinion of the way I looked. I was embarrassed, simple as that! So embarrassed in fact, that I'd even make excuses to avoid swimming in public. Especially if there happened to be lots of other kids around.

When I was younger, it was never an issue. I had always loved swimming and it was also something that I was quite good at. But at my first school swimming carnival a few years earlier, I noticed a lot of kids staring in my direction. At first, I thought they were surprised to see me win so many races and also that they were impressed by the number of ribbons I'd won.

But when I tuned into their thoughts, I found that what they were really thinking was very different to anything I could ever have imagined.

"Wow! She's so skinny!"

"Haha! Check out that girl. She's like a bean pole."

"OMG. That girl looks so bad. I'd hate to be that thin!"

Horrified at what I'd heard, I quickly threw my towel around my shoulders and raced to the bathroom to change. From that moment on, I pretended to be feeling unwell and refused to swim in any more races. All I wanted was to be left on my own in misery, away from the stares of the other kids.

Even though the teachers tried to encourage me to continue, there was no way that I could be coaxed back into the water. And when another girl was awarded the age champion medal instead of me, I didn't care. No medal was worth the humiliation of kids staring at me the way they had done.

What hurt the most, however, was the mean, ugly thoughts that had filled their heads.

That was the beginning of my body conscious behavior. At least that's what my mom called it and in an effort to help, she would double the quantities of food in my lunch box each day and offer extra helpings for dinner. But regardless of how much I ate, I could not put on weight. Gradually I grew taller, but this only made me look lankier than ever.

Occasionally, I'd catch my mom watching me, her eyes filled with worried concern.

And I knew exactly what she was thinking.

"Emmie is so beautiful. Why can't she see it?"

But my mother's thoughts were very different to my own and I scoffed at the remarks racing through her head.

As I stood staring at my reflection that morning, I prayed for the hundredth time that my body would improve as I grew older.

Then, with the sudden realization that I was going to be late if I didn't hurry, I was forced to turn away from the vision in the mirror and quickly race out of my room. As I did, I happened to notice the photo that was taken of my dad and myself when I was little, and I instantly felt a familiar calming sensation take hold. It seemed that he always appeared when I needed him most and for that, I was truly thankful.

Brushing away all anxious thoughts, I headed quickly for the front door, a growing sense of excitement causing the smile to return to my face.

After giving my mom another brief hug of thanks for the beautiful top that I was so grateful to have been given, I waved goodbye before disappearing from sight.

Right then, I forced all negative thoughts out of my head, choosing instead to focus on the image of the friendly girl waiting to meet me.

However, I was completely unaware of what was in store for me that day. Nor did I have any idea of the new power I would soon be capable of.

This discovery would be the beginning of some unforeseen events. And right then, if anyone had tried to warn me, I would not have believed them.

The discovery...

Sitting in the booth of a burger bar a few hours later, Millie and I continued to laugh and chat as we munched on the food in front of us. We seemed to have so much in common and several of Millie's favorite things were exactly the same as my own; the same food, the same songs and even the same movies. Although we'd only known each other for a short time, it was so easy to hang out with her, almost as if we'd been friends forever. I was also aware that she felt exactly the same way about me.

I'd made sure not to comment or give any indication I knew what she was thinking, but it was great to know that I'd finally made a real friend. Right then I was the happiest girl alive.

As we sat eating our lunch, an idea appeared abruptly in my mind. I had no clue at all as to where it had come from, but I knew instinctively that it was the key. I had to control my powers. If I didn't, my life would continue to be a misery and that was something I definitely wanted to avoid. I was also prepared to try anything in order not to ruin the friendship that was forming between Millie and myself.

For me to read minds, all I had to do was concentrate on a person's thoughts. But why not reverse that power and focus on blocking them instead?

The idea seemed so simple, I couldn't understand why I hadn't thought of it before. However, the only way I'd know if it would work was to give it a try. And I decided that right then was as good a time as any.

Millie was in the middle of telling me about the band she'd formed the year before with her friends, Julia, Blake, and Jack and I was amazed to hear that she had actually been the lead singer. It sounded such a cool thing to do and I tried my best to listen carefully to every detail.

At the same time, I began to build an invisible brick wall in my mind. Although it took a huge amount of effort to concentrate on the two tasks at once, I found that if I focused hard enough, it was possible to listen to Millie's conversation and create the wall as well.

Obviously, the wall didn't really exist, it was just a figment of my imagination, kind of like an invisible barrier inside my head. But instead of blocking Millie's face from view, all it blocked were her thoughts. And as the seconds ticked by, I realized that with each brick added, the weaker my power became. Until, at last, all I could hear was the sound of the words coming directly from Millie's moving lips. The thoughts in her head remained hers and hers alone.

For me, this discovery seemed a miracle of huge proportions. It was a serious breakthrough and although it needed intense concentration, it was definitely worth the effort.

Up until then, I'd spent most of my time pushing people away; simply because they found me too weird. But I was sure that if I could master this skill then my problems would be over.

When Millie hopped up to find the bathroom, I decided to test my discovery on the man sitting in the booth next to ours. He was facing my way and the perfect target to practice on. But before I had a chance to start, his thoughts unexpectedly found their way inside my mind; passing through as clearly as if he were sitting right next to me.

"I reckon I can grab that wallet. Probably the phone too. That stupid girl is so busy talking, she won't even notice."

Paying closer attention, I began to concentrate more intensely. I also took in his unusual appearance. Even though it was the middle of summer, he had the collar of his long sleeved coat standing up stiffly around his neck. And his unshaven face reminded me of a sinister cartoon type character; the typical stereotype of a robber or thief and I wondered briefly if all thieves tended to look that way. His hair was greasy and unwashed and he had smears of dirt across his cheeks. I guessed he might be a homeless person of some sort, but I could not feel sorry for him, not after realizing what he was up to.

His eyes darted back and forth towards the table across the aisle from mine, where I could see a group of teenage girls deep in conversation. And on the very edge was sitting the wallet that he was planning to steal. At the same time, the girls were so engrossed in each other, they were unaware of anything going on around them.

"This'll be easy! All I've got to do is grab it as I go past."

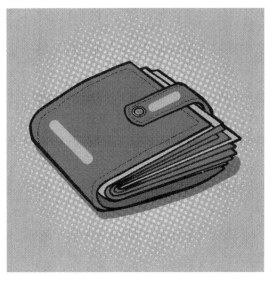

The voice in my head was more of a snarl and I could feel my skin crawl at the sound of it. But he must have felt me watching him because his gaze abruptly turned towards me.

Like a cornered rat, he seemed alert to everything going on around him and with a start, I wondered for a moment if he was picking up on what I was thinking. It was a disturbing thought but I forced myself to brush it away. I knew that if I didn't act fast, it would be too late. At the same time though, I didn't want to draw attention to myself. However, I could think of no other option.

Without stopping to consider the consequences, I stood up as if to head towards the front counter, but when I stepped into the aisle, I pretended to stumble over an unseen object on the floor. Grabbing hold of the girls' table for support, I nudged the wallet and phone away from the edge.

Instantly, the entire group of girls looked at me with concern, asking if I were okay. While they were all distracted, I discreetly pushed the objects further into the middle of the table. Then, turning back to my seat, I sat back down in my original spot. The girl sitting closest gave me an odd look, but in the spur of the moment it had been all I could think of; apart from declaring to the entire café that the dirty looking man sitting opposite was a thief.

Unfortunately, he had watched my every move and when I looked his way, our eyes locked in place. His intense stare was full of disgust and all I could do was stare guiltily back.

I could hear every word, every thought that filled his head and my stomach churned at the foul language he was directing towards me. But I kept my eyes fixed on him, even though his evil glare was causing the hairs on my arms to stand on end.

Without warning, he was on his feet, moving with the stealth of a prowling animal, hunting its prey. The items he'd intended to steal were beyond his reach but he paused beside me and scowled angrily while I sat deathly still in my place. Too scared to move, all I could do was stare back and hope that he would keep walking.

"Don't ever do that again!"

This time he spoke aloud and then he was gone.

With a quick glance behind me, I caught sight of his distinct figure as he made his way through the crowd just outside the café. And with my pulse racing, I smiled weakly at Millie who had just slid back into her seat opposite mine.

"Are you feeling okay?" she asked with a frown. "You look really pale."

"I think I just need some fresh air," I replied, taking a deep breath.

Following along close behind her as we made our way to the nearby exit of the shopping complex, I scanned the area anxiously hoping that the man was nowhere in sight.

He was one person I did not want to meet again and I struggled to shake away the scene I had just left behind.

What worried me most though, was the uneasy feeling that remained in the pit of my stomach and I looked quickly around, almost sure that I could feel him watching me.

Later that night as I lay in bed, tossing and turning and unable to sleep, I replayed the event over in my head.

While I was grateful to be able to help the girl, even though she had no idea of how close she had been to her things being stolen, I knew it was an experience I could have done without.

For me, reading people's minds constantly led to problems and I was still feeling very uneasy about what had happened that afternoon.

I knew that my mom called my mind reading ability a gift and said I should put it to good use, but all it seemed to do was get me into trouble. I'd had enough. I really could not deal with it any longer. And I decided right then that I must do what I could to make my life easier. I'd discovered a way to block any and all thoughts around me and I must find a way to practice that skill so it became a habit.

I also knew that it was up to me to make that happen.

New friends…

Millie and I had begun to hang out regularly. She was definitely the funniest and nicest girl I had ever met and I constantly found myself in hysterics over her random comments. If she was busy doing other things and we couldn't catch up then we'd simply text or direct message each other on Instagram.

My mom had bought me a mobile phone for my 12th birthday but I'd never used it much before, as I had no friends to contact. Since meeting Millie though, it was constantly making a pinging sound as we texted each other back and forth.

I was extremely grateful to have made such a nice friend but there was just one problem. As the days went by, something that didn't bother me at first, gradually became more and more of an issue. While I realized I should not be complaining, I found it hard to ignore.

Try as I might, I could not come to terms with Millie's constant chatter about her friend, Julia. It seemed that she was always being reminded of her and in just about every conversation, she mentioned her name.

"Julia loves doing that."

"Julia is so funny! She always cracks me up."

"I wish Julia were here so I could ask her opinion."

"Julia and I have been best friends for so long! I can't believe she doesn't live here anymore!"

"Julia, Julia, Julia…"

While I understood that they were very close and Millie was still getting used to not having her around, the fact that she could not stop talking about her had become a little annoying and more than a little upsetting.

Although Millie and I had only recently met, I desperately wanted her to think of me as her bestie. An actual close friend who I could tell all my secrets to was something I'd never had. While I knew there was one secret I could never share, I still wanted someone who thought of me as their best friend. However, when she invited me to her house one day, I was able to see first-hand how close she and Julia actually were.

On her bedroom shelves sat a heap of pretty photo frames and most of them contained pics of the two girls together. In each and every one, they both wore a beaming smile and it was obvious how much fun they'd had when they were together. While I couldn't help but feel a little envious, I began to understand how difficult it must have been for Millie when Julia had left. It also made me wonder how Julia was coping without Millie.

There was a great shot of the two of them sitting side by side on the front step of a house. Julia had her arm draped loosely around Millie's shoulder and the pair seemed completely content. With her head tilted and her eyes crinkled with amusement, Julia gazed into the distance. Millie was looking at Julia and laughing happily. The pair were obviously enjoying a funny moment together, their pose completely natural as they focused on each other and whatever it was they had shared, the two of them completely unaware of the camera.

Julia's big brown eyes and long dark hair were set off beautifully by the pretty pink top she was wearing, while Millie's blue T-shirt contrasted with it perfectly.

It really was a gorgeous photo and gave a true impression of how close they were.

Another picture showed the two of them dressed up in really cool Halloween outfits. They both looked amazing and I thought about how much fun that night must have been.

As I continued to scan the frames, stopping to admire each photo individually, my eyes fell upon one that immediately caught my interest. Rather than just the two girls, there were a couple of boys in the shot as well. One of them wore a cheeky grin while the other was making a funny face as he stared into the camera. I took in every detail of that photo, especially the close friendship amongst them. I then tried picturing myself as part of that group with my own face taking the place of Julia's.

"This is such a great shot, Millie." I smiled admiringly as I looked towards her. "Are these the boys in your band?"

"Yes they are!" she exclaimed, as she jumped up from her place on the bed. "Good guess, Em. That one is Blake and the one with the silly expression is Jack. He's always joking around!"

"It's such a cool photo," I replied. "And they're both so good looking!"

She laughed in response. "Yeah, I used to think so too. Well, I still think that Blake is. But he's Julia's boyfriend," she added before continuing. "I used to have a huge crush on Jack but that was a long time ago. We're just friends now."

"Wow!" I exclaimed with interest. "I can see why you liked him. He's really cute."

Millie grinned before replying. "There's another boy I had a crush on before school ended. I was hoping to bump into him over the summer, but so far I haven't seen him around at all. His name's Alec. And he's *really* good looking!"

Laughing in response, I could not help my next comment, "So many good looking boys in Carindale, Millie!"

And then, as I stared more closely at the photo, another thought occurred to me, "Poor Julia! She must really miss Blake!"

I was finding it hard to understand how she could leave someone like that behind. But then, as Millie had already told me, she had no choice. Her dad was starting a new job and they all had to move whether they wanted to or not.

"Yeah, she misses him heaps," Millie agreed, "But they call each other almost every night. So I guess that helps."

Staring more intently at the photo, Millie recalled the day it was taken. "That was when we all went to the local theme park. I think it was one of the best days I've ever had!"

I watched her as she focused on her memories. Then, without warning her smile abruptly disappeared, and for a moment I felt sure she was going to cry. When she turned her back on me, I searched for something to say; anything to help her feel better.

"Maybe we could do something fun together, Millie? And maybe you could even introduce me to some of your friends. I'd love to meet them."

I held the group photo in my hand and hoped she'd pick up on the hint I was trying to make. Then, turning to me with a smile, I could see her eyes brighten.

"I'll give Blake a call tonight and see what they're up to," she replied eagerly, all traces of sadness disappearing from her face. "That would be a lot of fun, Em and I'm sure you'll like them!"

"Sounds great," I replied happily, and at the same time, I tried to contain the excitement I felt bubbling inside.

I didn't want to appear too enthusiastic about the idea of meeting Blake and Jack but it seemed that things were heading in the right direction. For me, having a group of cool people to hang out with would be a dream come true and although Millie missed Julia terribly, I knew that we were gradually becoming good friends. It would probably take some time, but that was okay. I would just have to be patient.

Later that night when I was in bed and trying to sleep, I realized something else had also taken place during my visit to Millie's. For the first time since we started hanging out together, I had not read her thoughts, not even once. Although tempted at one stage, I controlled myself and focused on building a wall in my mind instead.

It was something I'd been practicing on my mom and was gradually becoming better at. I could also see that each time I practiced, it became quicker and easier than the time before. Hopefully soon, it would be automatic. That was what I needed to aim for.

As I replayed the events of the day, I also recalled the group photo I'd spent so much time admiring, and once again, a flutter of excitement took hold in my stomach. To be part of a group, just hanging out and having fun, especially with Millie and the two boys in that picture, was definitely something to look forward to.

With that thought foremost in my mind, I finally drifted into a deep sleep. And when I woke the next morning, I was sure that my smile from the night before was still fixed firmly in place. The feeling of excitement was quite new to me, but I was certainly enjoying the sensation and I could barely wait to hear what Millie had arranged. With the smile still intact, I made my way into the kitchen for breakfast.

Uneasy...

As it turned out, I did not see Millie at all for the next two weeks and for that matter, I barely heard from her either. Apparently, her grandmother was unwell and she had gone with her mom to help care for her. Then, just when I thought she was heading home again she was invited to stay with her cousins for a week. Hugely disappointed, I tried to keep busy and focus on the fun we would have together when she finally arrived back.

But I found it hard to be patient. I was so looking forward to meeting her friends and as well as that, I'd already become used to spending most days with her. Not having her around made me feel lonelier than ever and it was not a nice feeling at all.

I was also disappointed by her lack of texts. Although I'd sent several messages, I'd only received a few replies in return. Deep down, I knew that she was busy and probably didn't have time to be on her phone texting me. But it made me feel that I was much lower on her priority list than she was on mine. As much as I tried not to think that way, I couldn't help it.

However, after a couple of days of moping around the house, I received another message from Millie, explaining that she'd be back at the end of the week. Realizing that I'd been overreacting, I decided to find some things to do until she returned.

In a much better frame of mind, I decided to join my mom on a trip to the city. It was one place we had not yet visited and the day became even better when she suggested we check out the huge range of clothing shops on offer.

That, of course, was the best part and the two of us ended up coming home with several new outfits. In particular, I especially loved the new black jeans that I'd found at one of the designer jeans stores but even after a whole day of shopping, I still hadn't found a top to match; there was a certain style that I was looking for but hadn't been able to find anything close.

One afternoon a few days later, I decided to wander down to the local mall to see if anything caught my eye. As it turned out, that day the area was extremely busy. Being summer holidays, there were lots of people about; parents with children, kids around my age, and teenagers hanging out and looking for something to do. I also discovered some free entertainment. As well as a couple of buskers, singing and playing instruments in the middle of the mall, there was a really cool street performer who was set up in a small amphitheater. He was performing on a circular stage area while all the spectators sat on the tiered steps that led down towards it.

His act had attracted a large audience and their cheering caught my attention. Deciding to stay and watch, I searched for a place to sit and then looked on while he set alight a number of juggling sticks and tossed them into the air, the flames soaring high into the sky. He then repeated his show by juggling a variety of odd shapes, all of this was done while riding around on a huge unicycle. This was a clever thing to do on its own, without having to juggle at the same time.

As well as his tricks, he was also a very funny comedian and the crowd was soon in fits of laughter. But when he moved onto his magic act and scanned the audience in search of a volunteer, I certainly did not expect to be the one chosen.

When I realized he was pointing at me, I stared towards the ground and then at the people around me, hoping I was mistaken. When I didn't respond, I prayed that he'd overlook me and move onto someone else. I was not so lucky and when he called out loudly for the girl in the striped red and white T-shirt to come down and join him, I had no choice but to do as he'd asked.

I had no idea why he'd chosen me, especially as there was a stack of kids with their hands raised, desperate to be picked. Then I realized that it was all part of the act. He'd managed to gain the audience's attention and have everyone laughing at what he considered to be a funny joke, but it made me feel more awkward than ever. With their loud cheers encouraging me to take part, I was forced to make my way down the steps to the stage area below, all the while my face turning as red as the stripes on my T-shirt.

Making the situation even worse was a group of teenage boys who continued to cheer and whistle. Along with their yelling and cheering, they were making rude remarks. With every pair of eyes directed towards me, I was forced to stand by the performer's side. I desperately wished I could return to my seat.

All I could do though was look anxiously on as the performer shuffled a deck of very large, oversized playing cards and placed them in 3 separate piles on a table in front of us. He then demonstrated his trick by securing a thick, black blindfold around my head and selecting a random card that he then showed to the audience. Although I could not see a thing through the blindfold, I knew exactly what was going on in the performer's mind. The calling and cheering from the group of boys had continued and in my embarrassed state, I was alert to everything going on around me.

My mom and I often played card games together and I was familiar with all the card names. Completely flustered and without thinking about what I was doing, I abruptly blurted out the name of the card in his hand.

"It's a red Queen of Diamonds."

"She guessed the card," called a man sitting nearby. "She must be able to see through the blindfold."

The performer looked towards me with a frown, obviously thinking that I'd peeked. He was then forced to check the blindfold was secured properly and demonstrate the trick again.

More embarrassed than ever, and finding it hard to believe that I had just announced the correct card name to the entire crowd, I purposely called out the wrong details next. The performer then repeated the trick himself, and after covering his own eyes with the blindfold was able to name the exact card that I'd chosen. This, of course, was all part of his magic act but I knew he was relieved when it was finally over and he was able to ask me to leave the stage.

With a confused and curious expression, he thanked me for participating. Still feeling embarrassed, I could not help but murmur a rude reply, "It's your fault! You shouldn't have chosen me in the first place!"

Ignoring the frown that appeared on his face, I made my way quickly back up to street level, at the same time, the cheers and whistles from the group of boys ringing loudly in my ears.

Keen to get as far away as possible, I headed through the crowded mall towards some fashion stores that I knew were situated at the other end. Standing outside one of the shops, I scanned the window display, wanting to catch my breath and try to forget about what had just happened. I had certainly not expected to become part of an embarrassing magic act when I'd left my house a couple of hours earlier.

Thankfully though, I noticed a pink midriff top hanging in a corner. Finally, able to put the incident behind me, I focused on the pretty top instead.

Staring at it some more, I tried to decide how it would look with my new jeans but then, unexpectedly, something else in the window happened to catch my attention.

With the bright sunlight shining on the glass, all I could see was a dark shape and at first, I thought it might be one of the teenagers from the amphitheater. But then I realized that the shape towered over my own reflection and was way too tall to be a kid. I'm not sure why it stood out but for some reason, I felt drawn to it.

As well as my ability to read people's minds, I had what my mom called the sixth sense. It wasn't completely reliable but right then, the familiar prickly feeling at the base of my neck was telling me that I definitely had something to worry about.

Turning abruptly, I found myself face to face with the one person I had hoped never to see again and I felt an instant chill work its way down my spine. Even though it was a warm and sunny afternoon, the goose bumps that appeared on my arms were causing me to shiver.

Wearing the same dark overcoat with the collar once again standing upright around his neck, the familiar but creepy figure did not budge from his spot. Instead, he stood staring back at me; the dark intense eyes, causing the hand of fear to claw at the pit of my stomach.

Where had he come from and what did he want? They were the questions racing through my head. But I did not dare to stop and focus on his thoughts. All I wanted was to get away as quickly as possible.

Breaking into a run, I headed out of the mall and down the street and I did not glance back until I was quite a distance away.

A quick look behind assured me that he was no longer in sight and apart from a few people heading in the direction of the mall and some passing cars, there was no one else around.

Regardless, my heart continued to pound in my chest and I could feel its strong rhythm all the way to my front gate, where I was finally able to take a deep breath of relief.

When I raced up the front steps of the house, the door swung wide open and I stared in surprise at my mom, who was just about to head out the door.

"Where are you going?" I panted anxiously.

"I have to pick up some groceries for dinner," she replied with a frown. "Em, are you alright? You look like you've seen a ghost!"

"I'm okay. But I think I'll come with you!"

As grocery shopping was one thing I did not enjoy, she was certainly not expecting to hear those words from me. "Are you sure about that? Are you not feeling well, Emily?"

My mother only called me Emily if I was in trouble or there was a problem. And clearly she was expecting some type of explanation to help her understand why I'd suddenly be interested in grocery shopping, the thing I complained about most and usually tried to avoid.

"I'm just tired of being at home on my own," I lied, shooting her a quick grin as I headed back down the steps.

Reaching to open the door of the car, I jumped quickly inside, hoping to avoid any more questions. The last thing I wanted was to worry her when there was more than likely a reasonable explanation.

Thinking some more about what had just happened, I considered all the details. The mall and shopping area were a perfect target for a thief, and that strange man probably hung out there regularly. There was sure to be an endless supply of distracted shoppers to steal from and I convinced myself that the chance meeting had been pure coincidence.

Perhaps he remembered me from the café and wanted revenge by giving me a scare. Well, he'd certainly done that and I hoped never to cross paths with him again.

As much as I wanted to believe that story though, I could not shake the feeling that there had to be something more.

Why had he stopped to stare at my reflection in the window?

And the evil glare he gave me when I turned to face him had made my skin crawl. He seemed to be looking into my soul, searching inside for answers. But answers to what?

I tried to push my next thought away but it was not easy. Especially because my intuition was telling me that the mysterious man in the shopping mall might be a mind reader as well.

Could it be at all possible?

Were there other people like me, people with the same powers and the same abilities?

And if that were the case, then why did he behave that way? It just did not make sense.

Sighing in frustration, I thought of my dad.

"What's going on, Dad? Please help me figure this out," I whispered the words silently in my head.

But for once this did nothing to ease my mind.

As hard as I tried, I was unable to ignore the familiar prickle that had once again appeared at the base of my neck.

The uncomfortable chill was working its way through my body and making me more uneasy than ever.

Excitement...

That evening, I helped Mom to prepare dinner. This was something I often did but on that night, in particular, it was a good distraction. Mom was trying out a new recipe and already the aroma coming from the pot on the stove was making my mouth water.

Completely focused on my job of peeling and chopping potatoes, the pinging sound of a text on my phone caught me by surprise. When I glanced at the screen and saw that it had come from Millie, I grabbed the phone in the desperate hope she had arrived back home.

"Good news? Mom asked as she eyed me curiously.

I looked towards her, the grin spreading wide on my face as I squealed loudly with delight. Millie had returned that afternoon and was inviting me to the movies the following day. That in itself was awesome news but what made it really special was the fact that Millie had been in contact with Jack and Blake and they were keen to go as well. It seemed that my wish was coming true and I could feel the joy inside me bubbling to the surface.

However, when I shared the news with Mom, I certainly did not expect the frown that appeared abruptly on her face.

"Who are Jack and Blake?"

Just as I opened my mouth to explain, she quickly interrupted.

"I'm glad to hear that you're making friends, Emmie, but I'm not happy about you heading off to the movies with a couple of boys I've never heard of.

You haven't even mentioned them before. How do you know them and where are they from?"

"They're good friends of Millie's?" I stammered anxiously, gulping at the possibility of not being allowed to go.

"She's been friends with them for ages and she said they're really nice."

My mother's frown deepened as she looked at me suspiciously and I could see her brain ticking over. Anxious to know what was going on in her mind, I broke into her thoughts and alarm bells instantly started to ring in my own head.

She was wondering what I'd been up to that day and did not believe that I'd been hanging out at the mall on my own after all. I could feel my stomach drop as I realized she was planning to make me stay at home.

"Mom, come on!" I cried in exasperation. "I went to the mall to watch the street performers today and then I did some window shopping. That's all! Surely you're not going to say no!"

There was no way I wanted to mention anything else that had happened but I had to convince her to let me go to the movies. She had to let me go! She just had to!

"Jack and Blake are the boys from Millie's band," I continued, desperate to persuade her. "I already told you about the band she formed with her friend, Julia. You're always going on about me making some new friends. Now here's my chance. I can't believe you'd say no."

"And besides," I added quickly. "I'm twelve years old now. I'm not five anymore and you know I can look after myself!"

Her expression began to soften but she was still unsure.

"Em, I want you to stay safe. It's just the two of us and if anything happened to you, I don't know what I'd do."

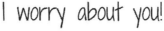

With a sigh, I moved towards her and gave her a firm hug. "Mom, nothing is going to happen to me. Moving here has been the best thing we've ever done. You said so yourself. I'm just going to the movies. It's no big deal. And I'll come straight home afterward if that's what you want."

I could see she was on the verge of agreeing but I could not risk the chance that she would still say no.

"If it makes you feel any better, you can drop me off and pick me up."

My pleading tone and final suggestion were the clinchers and I breathed a deep sigh of relief when she finally nodded her head.

"Alright, Emmie. I guess I have to let you grow up sometime. It's just happening too quickly!"

With the smile returning to my face I gave her another big hug of thanks then moved happily back to my spot at the kitchen bench. I tried to refocus on the potatoes I was chopping but could think of nothing else except the image of the two boys in Millie's photo. I could barely wait to meet them and I was sure they'd be every bit as nice as Millie had promised.

As well, I could not hide the fact that I found Jack very cute. I knew that Millie thought Blake was better looking but in my opinion, Jack was the one who stood out. There was something about his cheeky grin that I kind of adored and I was especially looking forward to meeting him.

Then, out of the blue, I realized I would have to decide on something to wear. Instantly, of course, the pink midriff top that I'd spotted that afternoon came to mind and I wished that I'd had the chance to buy it.

Out of all my new clothes, my jeans and that top would probably be the prettiest outfit of all. But at least I did have other new things to choose from.

When dinner was over and I'd helped with the dishes, I was able to go to my room and decide. After trying on a couple of different combinations I decided on a white flared skirt and a pink top that had a pretty sequined love heart pattern on the front.

I noticed as I stared at my reflection in the mirror that the skirt kind of camouflaged how thin my legs were. Perhaps that style was best for me; either that or my mom's huge meals were finally having an effect.

Whatever the reason, I was able to climb into bed feeling happier than ever. The following day could not come quickly enough and the image that came to mind was similar to the one in Millie's photo frame. Except for one important detail.

Julia's face was replaced by my own.

Unexpected...

When I arrived at the cinema the next afternoon and found Millie waiting impatiently near the entrance, I could barely control my excitement.

Giving her a quick hug, I exclaimed with delight. "It's so good to see you!"

"You too, Em!" she grinned in return. "I'm so happy you could make it today! But I've got some bad news. The boys can't come!"

At the sound of her words, my smile instantly disappeared.

"Blake's grandparents turned up at his house this morning so he had to stay at home. And Jack didn't want to come without him."

I could feel my face fall; hugely disappointed, I could not believe what she had just told me.

"Oh, no!" I cried in dismay. "I was really looking forward to meeting them."

"Yeah, I know!" Millie replied. "I was looking forward to you meeting them as well. It's not fair Blake's grandparents decided to show up today! I was going to suggest we try for another day, but I it sounds like he has a lot of family stuff on right now. So I guess we'll just have to wait."

Trying hard to hide my disappointment, I reminded myself that at least I was still able to spend time with Millie, and I knew I should feel grateful for that.

In an effort to cheer me up, she continued, "Don't worry. We'll see them another time.

We have the whole summer, remember?"

Giving my arm a quick squeeze, she smiled, "And besides, it gives me a chance to hang out with you. I've just had the most boring two weeks of my life and I'm so glad to be back!"

Following Millie to the ticket booth, I looked towards her curiously. From the texts she'd sent me, I had the impression she was having a great time while she was away, but I guessed I was wrong.

"You didn't have fun with your cousins?" I asked, a look of surprise on my face.

"Well, usually we have a great time together, but since they've moved to their country property, they've suddenly become obsessed with horses. I don't know where that came from because they've never even mentioned horses to me before. Now, horses are all they think about."

"Oh, wow!" I was more surprised at Millie's reaction than I was at anything else. To me, horses were amazing animals and I'd always dreamed of owning one. But it was clear that Millie wasn't interested in them at all.

"There's a fourteen-year-old girl who lives on the property next door and she has a couple of horses. Anyway, all they want to do is spend all day, every day at her place and now they're planning to get horses of their own. They don't talk about any else!" She rolled her eyes in disgust, clearly not happy about the situation.

"You obviously don't like horses, Millie!" I laughed in response.

This was one thing we did not have in common but her expressions were so funny, I couldn't help laughing.

"I'm kind of scared of them," she admitted abruptly, a serious frown appearing on her face.

In my mind, horses were the most beautiful creatures on the planet, so I found it hard to comprehend what she was saying.

"When I was nine, I went on a trail ride," she explained slowly. "It was my friend's birthday and there was a group of us. Everyone was really excited; all except me that was. I was feeling pretty nervous and I guess the horse I was riding picked up on that."

I followed Millie's words carefully, all the while, picturing the scene in my head.

"Anyway, my horse started trotting and I got scared and began to scream. The instructor told me later that my screaming must have spooked him because he took off through the bush. And all I could do was try to hang on!"

"Oh my gosh, that would have been terrifying!" I replied.

"It's a wonder you didn't fall off! And you could've been really badly hurt!"

"I know," she replied with a sigh. "But I've never been on a horse since that day. And I don't think I'll be going back to my cousins' house in a hurry, either!"

I looked at her sympathetically, finally able to understand how she must feel. Although deep down, I still hoped that one day I might have a horse of my own.

At that point, however, we had finally reached the front of the queue and were able to buy our movie tickets. With that distraction, I thought our talk of horses would be over. But as we headed towards the cinema entrance, Millie had some more unexpected news to share.

"The worst part is that Julia is now getting a pony as well. I can't believe it! For the last two weeks, that's all she's talked about. Every time she rings me, it's horses, horses, horses. I was looking forward to visiting her but now I'm not so sure. Seriously, why am I surrounded by people who are obsessed with horses all of a sudden?

Then, eyeing me curiously, she continued, "Please don't tell me you plan to move to the country and get a horse too!"

Laughing in reply, I shook my head.

"To be honest, I'd love to have my own horse. But I can guarantee that's not going to happen; especially not anytime soon!"

"Thank goodness for that," she grinned.

I followed her thoughtfully through the door and into the darkness of the cinema beyond.

Her sudden comment about Julia was surprising because she was previously so excited at the idea of visiting her; so much so that I'd become tired of hearing Julia's name constantly being mentioned.

It also seemed strange that I'd been wishing for Millie to stop dwelling on Julia, and instead, start focusing on her new friendship with me. Then all of a sudden, it seemed my wish might have come true.

Funnily enough, at that moment, I had no idea of another wish I'd been hoping for that was soon to become a reality as well.

And after my earlier disappointment, it came about much, much sooner than I had anticipated!

Feelings...

After the movie ended, Millie suggested we go for a wander through the mall and grab something to eat. Thankfully my mom had replied to my earlier text and agreed for me to stay out longer, which was great because I wanted to show Millie the midriff top I'd been eyeing off the day before.

While I still felt anxious about bumping into the creep who had scared me so much, I was determined that he would not stop me from having fun. As well, because I was with Millie I felt much safer than if I were on my own.

As it turned out Millie absolutely loved the top when I showed it to her in the store window. Then, when I tried it on along with a pair of jeans similar to the new ones I had recently bought, she insisted immediately that I should get it.

"Millie, that top looks stunning on you! And are those jeans the same as the ones you said you bought in the city?

When I nodded in reply, she exclaimed, "They're gorgeous! I'd like a pair like that myself."

Coming from Millie, this was a huge compliment. She had the most beautiful clothes and every time I saw her, she was wearing something really pretty. For her to compliment me on my choice of clothes was such a good feeling.

She'd already commented earlier on the outfit I was wearing that day as well, and instantly, her words had put a huge smile on my face.

"Ooh, I love your outfit, Emmie! Where did you get your skirt? It looks so good on you!"

But it was the comment she made as I headed towards the shop counter with the midriff top in my hand that was the most special of all.

"You have the best figure, Emmie. You're so lucky!"

"What?" I replied, the shock causing me to repeat my question. "Who, me?"

"Yes, of course, you!" she laughed with a shake of her head. "Who else would I be talking about?"

Speechless and lost for words, I was unsure how to respond. No one had ever said anything like that to me before; except my mom that was. But my mom's comments didn't really count.

Because of the way I felt about my body, I was finding it hard to believe that Millie really meant what she had said, and although I'd promised myself several times that I would respect her privacy, this was one occasion where I could not resist checking to be completely sure.

In the past, I'd met girls who would say things but not really mean them. And it hurt so much to have them smile to my face but at the same time think horrible, mean thoughts in their heads.

"Those types of people are what you call two-faced," my mom had explained to me later.

And I soon learned the meaning of that expression. Those girls had a face they showed on the outside that was the one that everyone saw. But at the same time, they had another one hidden away inside.

They said one thing but really meant another.

Thankfully though, Millie was different. It had only taken a second or two to read her mind and I had all the reassurance I needed. She seemed to say exactly what she was thinking. And it was her next thought that completely changed my life.

"I don't think Emmie has any idea of how pretty she is. And she's such a nice person! I'm so lucky to have her as my friend!"

When I heard those words silently spoken inside Millie's head, I did a double take and stared intently towards her. But she simply smiled back; that wonderful, genuine smile that I had come to know. And instantly my heart welled with happiness.

To Millie, I was not a gawky, skinny freak. I did, in fact, look good in the clothes I wore, and she was happy to have me as her friend.

Right then, I thought my day could not get any better.

But then as is sometimes the case, something completely unexpected happened.

And when I later thought about the chance meeting, I wondered if some things were just meant to be.

A crush...

Recalling his startled look of surprise as he stared at me then at Millie and back to me again, I was convinced that my heart had definitely skipped a beat.

Jack was the cutest looking boy I had ever come across. When I lay in bed that night and thought about the moment Millie and I had spotted him in the mall, I felt a small flutter in my stomach.

"Is that Jack?" I had asked Millie, as I tried not to stare in his direction.

He had been standing on the outskirts of a circle of families and kids being entertained by yet another street performer. This one, however, was a young rap singer, and the sound of his music had immediately caught our attention.

It had obviously caught Jack's as well and I watched him from a distance as he stood mesmerized by the teenager blasting out the words of the latest rap tune. It sounded so cool. The rhythm combined with the lyrics created a really catchy effect and the entire crowd was fascinated.

"OMG! It is Jack!" Millie responded with surprise. "That's amazing! How did you know it was him?"

Turning a slight shade of red, I did not want to admit that I'd been obsessing over his image from the day she had shown me the group photo; so much so that I had recognized him immediately.

The moment the rapper finished his song, Jack happened to turn our way, almost as though he could feel someone watching him.

That was when I caught sight of the brown eyes that had stood out so dramatically in the photo. But feeling the blush on my skin deepen, I looked quickly away.

"Oh my gosh. He saw me staring. How embarrassing!"

The words raced through my head while at the same time, I tried to comprehend the fact that he was right there in our midst.

Then, when Millie called out to him and he headed over, I could feel my stomach doing somersaults as I stood nervously by her side.

When Millie introduced me, I tried not to be awkward but I was struggling to act normally. He was even better looking in real life and I could not take my eyes off his cheeky grin.

He seemed to be staring at me as well and I wondered for a moment what he was thinking. Was it good or bad? Right then, I had to know and could not resist the temptation to find out. With the butterflies fluttering wildly inside me, I concentrated on his thoughts and instantly felt my face turn even redder.

"She's so pretty! Maybe I should've gone to the movies after all!"

Looking quickly away, I focused on Millie. Then in the next breath, I began to build the invisible brick wall in my mind, the one that I knew for sure, needed to be built as quickly as possible.

If I were going to have any chance of acting normally around him, I had to block his thoughts. But I needed help. For some reason, where Jack was concerned, the temptation to read his mind was just too much for me to control. And as I focused on piling the bricks, one on top of the other, I avoided all eye contact with the boy at my side.

A few minutes later, when I'd finally begun to relax, Millie suggested that we grab a table and something to eat. With the cheeky grin remaining fixed to his face, Jack instantly agreed. So we quickly found a place to sit and ordered our food.

Millie had not seen Jack since Julia had left town and obviously had lots to catch up on. This gave me the chance to listen in while the two of them reminisced about their last days of school before the summer break. They had shared so many memories with Julia and Blake and I could not help but feel envious about the fun things they'd all been a part of.

One, in particular, was their band. The fact that they'd been asked to perform at their graduation ceremony, seemed the coolest thing ever.

Watching the two friends as they chatted and laughed, I could see how special their years together at Carindale Middle School had been. Whereas my school life had passed by in a blur; too many schools, too many "fake" friends and too many sad memories.

If only my mom and I had moved to Carindale sooner, the previous years of my life could have been so different. But then I remembered about Julia, and I realized that the opportunity to become a part of this incredible group of friends would never have happened anyway.

As I lay on my bed later that evening thinking back over the afternoon, I thought again of Jack's smiling face and the constant laughter from all of us. He was one of the funniest people I'd ever met and apart from being extremely good-looking, he also seemed to be a really nice person.

But then another thought occurred to me, one that had crossed my mind earlier but had been brushed aside; probably because I didn't want to acknowledge it or believe that it might be true.

Millie had mentioned a previous crush. And although she said she didn't feel that way about Jack anymore, I wondered if that were really the case.

The two seemed to get on very well. Obviously, they'd been good friends for a long time, and it showed. They also had their singing in common and were now talking about catching up for a rehearsal to work on some of their old songs. There was an upcoming competition that Jack was planning to enter, and he was encouraging Millie to do the same.

According to Jack, Millie had an amazing voice and at the same time, Millie explained how awesome Jack was as a rapper. It was so great to see each of them encouraging the other. But was there really something more?

I'd never asked Millie about her friendship with Jack. She'd simply told me that Julia and Blake were going out and were still really close, even though she'd moved away. She had never given any other details and I hadn't asked.

I could feel my smile fading. The more I thought about the way Millie had acted around Jack, the more uneasy I felt.

There was a solution though. For me, it was quite simple.

My mom always said that I had powers for a reason.

And at least that way, I would know for sure what was really going on in my friend's head; and Jack's too for that matter.

When I pictured his cheeky grin as he said goodbye, I felt the small flutter in my stomach once again. I just hoped that I was wrong about Millie and that things could work out perfectly for me for a change.

Apart from a dorky looking kid who was nice to me back in fourth grade, I had never had a real crush on a boy.

At my last school, many of the girls in my class had boyfriends and all they'd talk about during their lunch breaks were boys.

In the end, I grew tired of it all and just tended to keep to myself. They preferred it that way though and were more than happy when I'd disappear to the library during lunch breaks.

But all of a sudden, I did have a boy to think about. And I was certain that even though we'd only just met, he quite liked me as well.

I then remembered that Millie's friendship was much more important to me than a silly crush. And when Jack's smiling face came to mind once again, I pushed the image out of my head.

All I could do was hope that things would work out in the end.

They just had to.

Millie's news...

When I saw Millie a couple of days later, it was at my house. I had originally hoped that we'd spend the afternoon together and then have a sleepover. But Millie had already planned to catch up with Jack for a rehearsal, so by the time she arrived it was late afternoon. As soon as I heard her knock, I raced to open the door and found her bouncing on the spot with excitement.

The competition was scheduled for the following month and both Millie and Jack had registered an entry in the solo division. It was the very first time for this event in Carindale and apparently, heaps of people of different ages were planning to take part. Millie blurted out all the details, her level of excitement rising with every word.

"Carindale's Got Talent" posters were popping up everywhere. And because of the overwhelming demand, they had decided to have two categories, one for younger kids and one for teenagers and adults.

As Millie and Jack were both thirteen, they were eligible for the 13 Years and under division, which was very lucky. Otherwise, they'd be competing against hugely talented people like the rapper we'd seen in the mall. Millie and Jack obviously had a much better chance against younger kids, although they would still be competing against each other.

But this didn't seem to bother either of them in the slightest. In fact, all they were concerned about was encouraging each other to do their best. It was all that Millie could talk about and her rehearsal with Jack that afternoon had made her more eager than ever.

When my mom overheard all the excited chatter coming from the living room, she sat down to join us, hugely interested in hearing about the competition Millie had entered. She was also interested in hearing Millie sing.

This had taken a little convincing, and at first, Millie refused, using the excuse, "I'm too shy!"

But I simply laughed off that remark because I knew for a fact, she was definitely not shy. Besides that, she had performed in front of large crowds before, including the whole of Carindale Middle School at her graduation. So, surely she could sing for my mom and me in the safety of our small living room!

While I was expecting that Millie would sound quite good, I was certainly not prepared for the voice that exploded from her lips when she began her song. She was singing along with the music that I had downloaded on iTunes and we could hear the words clearly through the speakers sitting in the corner of the room. However, it took only a few seconds for her to become more confident and then the music from the speakers was completely muffled by the power of her voice.

Sitting alongside my mom on the sofa, we both looked on in awe. My arms seemed to be covered in goose bumps and when I noticed the prickly feeling, I realized that the hairs on my arms were also standing on end.

The moment the song ended, the surprise on my mom's face was obvious in her voice as well. "Millie that was incredible!"

"Oh my gosh, Millie!" I squealed in shock. "You are amazing!!!"

Smiling broadly, she looked at each of us in turn. "Do you really think so?"

I could see that her question was genuine. Even though she must surely have been told endless times before that she had a great voice, she was still disbelieving. Or perhaps she was just being modest, but when we nodded our heads and raved about how much we loved the tone of her voice, she beamed happily with thanks.

"Sing something else," I begged. "Please, Millie. You are so good!"

"Yes, Millie, choose another song. This is fabulous!" My mom was clearly enjoying Millie's performance as much as myself, and I smiled widely at her reaction.

Millie grinned at the two of us and needed no further encouragement to begin another song, explaining that she needed help deciding which one to choose for the competition.

So we listened carefully, but it quickly became obvious that it was not an easy decision to make. While Mom liked the first, I thought that the second one sounded better. As it was one of my favorite top ten songs though, I was probably biased and we could not come to an agreement. Then I reminded Millie that she still had four weeks to decide.

But my mom continued prattling on about Millie's voice and other suggestions for songs that she might like to consider. I could see that she was not helping the situation and besides that, I was desperate to grab Millie and head to my room, so that we could have some time to ourselves.

My mother loved talking, probably because she spent her days on the computer and didn't often get the chance to meet people in person. Whenever she started speaking, it was always hard to get a word in.

She also loved asking questions; the most random things would sometimes come from her mouth and I'd often roll my eyes with embarrassment. Whenever I complained about her habit, she'd remind me that it was the only way to get to know a person.

That afternoon was no different. From the moment Millie had walked in the front door Mom had barely stopped talking. So I knew I had to step in. At the first opportunity, I caught Millie's attention and we eventually managed to slip away.

I was desperate to hear all about her afternoon at Jack's and could not get to my room quickly enough.

Jack's smiling face had been stuck in my head for the past two days and I wanted to reach into Millie's thoughts. That was my way of finding out about people, and I knew that it was often the only way to hear the truth. Asking questions, the way my mom tended to do, did not always work. Whereas my method was kind of foolproof.

As it turned out, I managed to find out a lot more information that I had previously anticipated.

Emotions...

It became immediately obvious that Jack had not only been on my mind but on Millie's as well. While this was to be expected, especially after they'd spent all afternoon rehearsing together, I could see that Millie's thoughts went even deeper.

Although I tried, I could not prevent the uncomfortable feeling of disappointment. But there was also something else. If I were to be completely honest, I'd be forced to admit there was another emotion I was feeling quite intensely right then. And it was one I'd become familiar with over the years.

On so many occasions in the past, I had stood back and watched other girls with their close knit groups; all such good friends, hanging out, doing fun stuff together, laughing, joking, sharing secrets, having fun. And there I was, the weird loner, or loser, I should probably say, on my own as usual.

Time and time again, I could not help the emotion that had forced its way to the surface. It wasn't nice and I wasn't proud of it. Regardless, however, I was unable to prevent it.

That emotion was a word beginning with the letter J.

A capital J.

And that's what I called it...the J word.

My mom told me once that Jealousy was a curse. And I found out for myself that she was right. Because jealousy made me miserable. And right at that moment, there it was again.

Only this time, it wasn't because I did not have a best friend to hang out with. I'd found a best friend but quite unexpectedly, something else had caused that cursed feeling to rear its ugly head once more.

And oddly enough, on this occasion, the Jealousy curse was having the exact same effect as it had in the past; a dark, sickly feeling in the bottom of my stomach and in the back of my head. I could feel the throbbing of its pulse as I sat listening to the words coming from Millie's mouth.

"Jack sounded so good today! You should've heard him, Emmie. His voice is even better than before."

"He's been practicing heaps and it really shows. I've already told him he's going to win. But he doesn't believe me. He's convinced that I'll win!"

"I love singing and so does Jack. It's awesome!"

Millie laughed happily, the delight obvious on her face. She could not stop talking about him and it did not take a mind reader to work out what she was thinking.

"Jack, Jack, Jack…"

I knew I should be happy for her. I knew that he was her friend. I also knew that they'd been friends forever. Whereas I had only just met him.

It was almost comical really; that I should feel so intensely about someone I had only met once and happened to spend a couple of hours with. But for some reason, we seemed to click. And I felt more comfortable with him than I had felt with anyone ever before. Perhaps even more so than with Millie.

"You're pathetic Emily!" I spoke the words harshly in my head, reprimanding myself for being such a loser.

"You've just met the guy and look at you! What a joke!"

And then, when I thought that things could not get any worse, Millie proceeded to share some more startling news.

And the wretched feeling in the pit of my stomach suddenly became much worse.

Shock...

"Jack and I came up with the most incredible idea!" Millie was so excited about her news and I sat on my bed trying to focus on her words, all the while attempting to ignore the sick feeling that was taking over my whole body.

"Carindale's Got Talent has become so popular they've decided to add a new category to each age group." Millie continued on with her spiel and I continued on with my efforts to follow what she was saying.

"Instead of combining all the solo and group performances together, they now have two sections, one for solo artists and one for groups. Apparently, there are a few dance troupes entering with twelve or more dancers in each. As well there's a couple of bands and some other group acts. So it wouldn't be fair for people on their own to compete against them."

She paused briefly to take a breath.

"Anyway, Jack came up with the idea of getting together with Blake and entering the group section. Blake is an incredible drummer and we sound so amazing when we perform together. And then I thought of the biggest brain wave. At first, I didn't think it would be impossible, but then I decided it wouldn't hurt to ask."

Pausing for effect, she added with a huge grin, "So I made a phone call."

Right then, I really did not want to hear all the details. So much talk about the competition that she and Jack were entering together was making me feel more Jealous than ever.

Millie had already asked if I wanted to enter. "Is there something you're good at Emmie? Something that you could do, so you could enter as well?"

If only she knew!

"Yes, I actually do have a talent, Millie. And my talent is so spectacular that I'm sure I would win!"

I imagined myself responding to her question. And I also imagined her look of disbelief as she listened to my answer. The idea of a genuine mind reader was too much for anyone to believe in. A person who could focus on the thoughts of any person at all in the audience, and share exactly what they were thinking…a color, a number, the time they went

to bed the night before, what they had for breakfast. You name it, a proper mind reader could tell you all the details.

And I was that person.

But could I enter a competition with my talent?

Of course not!

Refocusing on Millie's moving lips right then, I realized abruptly that she'd just said something I really should have been listening to.

"I made a phone call," she had said.

Those were her words but what had she said afterward….

It was something about Julia. Something that was making me more uneasy than ever.

So I asked her to repeat it.

"Sorry, Millie. I didn't catch that. Who did you decide to ring?"

And I listened as Millie's voice rose with excitement. She was so excited that she was on her feet, jumping up and down and almost bursting with joy.

I knew deep down that I should be excited too. I knew that I should feel happy for her.

But that prickly sensation at the base of my neck, the one I felt when I knew that something bad was going to happen, was making me feel otherwise.

And try as I might to join in her excitement, it was just not possible.

Changes...

The following evening, I received a call from Millie. And her news was exactly as I had expected.

"Emmie, Julia just called me back and guess what! She's allowed to come! Can you believe it? She asked her parents and at first, they said no. But then she begged and begged. She even told them she'd use her own savings to pay for the airfare. And it just so happens that there's a sale on flights right now. It's meant to be!"

Barely taking a breath, Millie continued, her voice becoming an excited jumble of words, "So now we'll be able to enter our band in Carindale's Got Talent. And you'll get to meet Julia, Emmie. You're going to love her; I know you will. This is the best news ever!"

She was practically screaming into the phone and I had to hold it away from my ear as she spoke.

"I almost didn't bother asking her, Em. She only left town a few weeks ago and I thought there'd be no way she'd be allowed to come back so soon. Plus, there's the pony thing that she's been so obsessed with. But she said she'll just put off getting a horse until she gets back. And because she's been missing us all so much and it's also the summer holidays, her parents finally gave in!!"

"That's so good, Millie." I tried to sound enthusiastic. I really did try, but I could not escape the sinking feeling that was taking hold.

Millie had talked about Julia so much and I was sure that she was every bit as nice as Millie said.

Julia...
she looked so nice in Millie's photos!

But what would she think of me?

And the one question I had not been brave enough to ask was, "How long is she staying for?"

If it were for the rest of the summer, then I was doomed. I just knew it.

To begin with, she was arriving in a few days and staying at Millie's house. She would be with her every single day and every single night. There'd be no time for me. And if I were Julia, I'm quite sure I wouldn't want to be sharing my best friend with some strange new girl who had recently moved into town and decided to take my place.

The photo of the four friends flashed into my thoughts.

Millie, Julia, Jack and Blake, standing side by side, best friends forever. And to think that I'd hoped to become a part of that group, and most importantly, to replace the girl who had left. What a pipe dream that was!

It was clearly not going to happen. Certainly not that summer anyway.

I'd been so excited about the weeks ahead. It was going to be the best summer I'd ever had. And then, almost overnight everything had changed.

Julia was due to arrive in a few days; not a few weeks, but a few days! Just my luck that the sale on airfares happened to be for that week only. The four friends would be reunited. And with the competition only a few weeks away they would spend their time rehearsing; as well as fitting in a heap of other fun stuff, I was sure.

And as for me?

Well, the picture I was painting in my head right then, was blank; an empty canvas. No color, no fun, no friends.

Just one lonely girl with a so-called miracle gift. One that was so miraculous it had to be kept intact, locked away in a secret place for safe keeping.

"You're so lucky to have that gift, Emmie." My mother's words rang in my head.

But right then, I would do anything to trade my gift for the one thing I truly wanted.

The one thing that had been within my grasp just the day before, to be whisked away once again.

Feeling thankful…

As I held the phone in my hand, something about Millie's tone made me refocus on what she was saying. I hadn't realized but she'd moved on from the excitement of Julia's arrival and was actually inviting me to hang out the next day.

I blinked a few times as a glimmer of hope registered in my mind.

Millie seemed aware of my thoughts and how I was feeling. Her reassuring words were reaching through the phone and although I was unable to read her mind right then, the message came through loud and clear.

She was not going to suddenly ditch me the moment Julia arrived. But instead, was already planning for us to meet and for the three of us to do some fun things together.

"I've told Julia all about you, Emmie, and she's really looking forward to meeting you! I'm sure you'll get on really well."

I listened carefully as she chatted on, my hopes beginning to soar. Maybe things would be okay after all. Perhaps I was spending too much time expecting the worst when it didn't need to be that way.

After all, up until the day before, I'd felt certain that Millie was a genuine friend. My gut instinct had told me so. For once in my life, I just needed to believe in myself. And I also needed to believe in Millie.

Then, as if to prove a point about her friendship being real, she was asking what I was up to the following day.

And a short while later, with an unexpected grin on my face, I found myself searching my cupboard for something suitable to wear.

Her invitation had come as a complete surprise. Totally unexpectedly, she had suggested we spend the day at one of the local theme parks. There were a couple of major ones nearby, I had seen them advertised on television. I'd certainly hoped to have the opportunity to go one day, but had definitely not expected it would be so soon.

And the idea that Millie was going to extra lengths to do something really fun with me before Julia arrived, was all I needed to put the smile back on my face. That meant more to me than anything.

That and the fact that she had two double passes which she could have saved for Julia's arrival; the two girls could easily have gone with Jack and Blake and I was certain that Julia would have loved that. But instead, Millie had decided otherwise.

She invited me for a sleepover at her house afterward and I quickly agreed.

After ending the call, I took a deep breath and glanced towards the photo of my dad that sat alongside my bed.

"Thanks, Dad!" I whispered quietly.

And as I looked lovingly into the eyes of the handsome man staring back, I knew that he was there.

He was with me every step of the way, I just needed to remember that, and everything would be okay.

Smiling gratefully at him once more, I turned back towards the cupboard to continue my search for the clothes I would need for the following couple of days.

Millie and her mom would be arriving early to pick me up and I wanted to be sure that I was ready.

An unexpected guest...

I had not been to a theme park since the time my mom took me for my sixth birthday. But at that stage, I was too young to go on all the big scary rides. I remember staring in awe as the roller coaster zoomed past us at break neck speed, the kids screaming and yelling as they clung tightly to the handrails.

To me, it was the most thrilling ride I could ever imagine and I dreamed of being able to ride it myself when I was old enough.

That day, my childhood dream came true. The roller coaster proved to be every bit as thrilling as I had imagined and just as I'd pictured in my head, I found myself clinging to the handrails in the exact same manner as the kids I'd watched when I was seven. And my screams were every bit as loud.

It was everything I'd hoped and when the ride ended, Millie and I raced towards the end of the queue so we could have another turn.

By the end of the day, we'd been on almost every scary ride we could find. It was the most fun I had ever had and when we hopped into Millie's mom's car later that afternoon, we were both bursting with stories about our fantastic day.

Just as we neared Millie's house, the sudden pinging noise from a text on her phone sounded loudly in the car. From my place alongside her on the backseat, I saw Jack's name appear in clear view on the screen. Quickly reading his message, she looked towards me with a grin.

"How would you feel about Jack coming over tonight? The other day he was complaining about being bored and I said he should come to my house for a movie and pizza sometime. But if you'd rather he didn't then that's fine, I'll just tell him to come another night."

"I don't mind at all," I replied smiling towards her.

"I didn't think you would," her grin widened as she asked her mom for permission to have one extra for dinner.

"That's fine, girls," Mrs. Spencer replied, in her usual cheery manner. "We'll just have to order extra pizza."

Looking towards Millie, I wondered curiously about what she'd just said. I really wasn't sure what she meant by that. But I had already promised myself to stay out of her head.

I had the invisible brick wall in place and I was determined that it should stay there. Millie was being such a good friend and she deserved that respect.

But then she made another comment about how much fun it was going to be when Jack arrived, and I really didn't need to read her mind to work out what she was thinking.

The dreamy look on her face as she smiled happily, said it all.

Truth...

As promised, Jack brought over a selection of movies. But all of them were action types and sci-fi, something we weren't expecting.

"Typical boy movies," Millie laughed as she looked through the pile.

We had cartons of pizza sitting on the glass-topped coffee table in front of us and were set up ready to go. All we needed to do was agree on a movie. In the end, we chose a latest release science fiction horror type, one that I was particularly interested in seeing because my mom had never let me watch anything other than PG movies before.

For me, this was going to be a first; not only the M rated movie but also the fact that I was having a sleep-over at a friend's house and a really cute boy was joining us for a few hours.

I'd already accepted the idea that Jack was Millie's friend and if she had a crush on him then I would just have to deal with it. There was no way I wanted to risk our friendship and besides, the two of them had so much in common, I guessed that they were destined to be together.

I kept my own crush hidden just below the surface, determined to keep it a secret. This was something I had experience with. I'd been keeping secrets my whole life, and this occasion was no different.

Thankfully, I'd also managed to hide away the cursed Jealous streak that I'd been attacked with a few days earlier. And rather than letting it fill me with pain and misery, I'd pushed it away right out of reach.

I could not help the fact that I liked Jack. He was so good looking and so much fun to be around. But Millie obviously thought so too. I just had to remind myself that her friendship mattered much more than a sudden boy crush.

One thing I had noticed though was his huge grin the moment he arrived and from that minute onwards, there had seemed to be a kind of connection between us. We really did get on extremely well; it was almost as though I'd known him forever.

Something told me that he felt it too. It was like an easy comfortable feeling that just seemed right. And if I had to keep my crush secret, at least I could try to enjoy simply hanging out with him as a friend.

Trying not to focus on the crush issue, I sat down alongside Millie, leaving room on the other side of her for Jack. She'd been drooling over him since he arrived and I did not want to get in the way. After dimming the lights a little, we settled down to watch the movie, all the while munching on the delicious pizza in front of us.

Throughout the film, Jack continued to startle both Millie and me; calling out and making loud noises right at the scariest moments, causing us to jump from our seats in fright. Laughing hysterically to himself, he sat prepared for each scary scene. As he had already seen the movie before, he knew exactly what was coming up next.

I was grateful for his humor though as it eased the tension in the room as well as the fact that I'd been clinging to my seat most of the time, unwilling to admit how scared I was.

Then, as soon as the movie ended, Millie stood up from her spot on the couch, brightened the lights and suggested we play a game instead.

"That's a great idea," I replied, smiling in agreement. I'd seen enough scary movies for one night and was more than happy to do something else. "What game do you have in mind?"

I was certainly not prepared for her response though and felt a small quiver of anxiety when she announced her choice.

"Truth or Dare!" she exclaimed excitedly, looking from Jack to me and back to him again.

"Sure!" Jack responded, "That sounds like fun!"

Hesitantly, I joined them on the floor as they sat cross-legged in the middle of the room. Although I'd heard of the game, I'd never played it myself, but for some reason, I felt slightly uneasy about what lay ahead.

The first few questions were quite harmless and within minutes we were all rolling around on the carpet in fits of laughter.

"Jack, I dare you to put on my mom's gardening hat then go downstairs and tell her how much you love it."

"What?" he replied, shaking his head in denial, as he stared in horror at the object sitting in view on top of a nearby cupboard. "She'll think I'm a freak! There's no way I can do that and keep a straight face."

"You have to!" she laughed. "It's my turn to give you a dare. And you have to do it!"

I joined in the laughter as we watched him put the large pink hat topped with fake flowers and other strange bits and pieces onto his head and make his way down the stairs.

It was one of the funniest things I'd ever seen and when he came back, his face bright red with embarrassment, I demanded that he put the hat back on so I could take a photo.

The game continued, with each of us giving each other crazy dares that made us all clutch our stomachs, the wild laughter creating sharp pangs of pain that we could not avoid.

But then the game turned more serious with Millie's next question. "Em, Truth…how old were you when you had your first kiss from a boy?"

Blushing deeply, I glanced back at her with a small shake of my head. "I've never been kissed by a boy."

I could feel Jack staring my way, but I did not return his gaze. The question was embarrassing but I think I was more embarrassed about having to admit that I'd never been kissed.

Instead, I looked down at the carpet, and fumbled through my brain, trying to think of a Truth question to ask him that wasn't quite so personal. Anything to change the subject and remove the attention from me.

"Jack, Truth...do you think Millie has a good voice?"

I grinned his way, knowing already what his answer would be. It was an easy question and he looked gratefully back as he answered. "I think Millie has an awesome voice!"

Alright, it's my turn again, Millie interrupted, as she turned quickly towards me, "Em, Truth...name the boy you have a crush on right now?"

Immediately feeling my face turns an even darker shade of red, I glanced quickly at Jack before looking at Millie once more.

How was I going to answer that? We'd all agreed to follow the rules and that meant being completely honest with our answers. But there was no way I could tell the truth. Why did Millie decide to ask me that?

But deep down inside I knew. She was aware of my feelings and once again, I felt convinced that she was able to reach into my thoughts as easily as I could reach into hers. Perhaps it was simply because we'd become close friends and she'd come to recognize what was going on in my head. Or was my face an open book? A place that showed all my inner most feelings, the ones that I desperately tried to keep secret.

Whatever it was, it was unnerving just the same.

And it gave me a very clear idea of how kids had felt in the past when they realized that I knew exactly what they were thinking.

Yes, it was creepy.

Yes, it was uncomfortable.

And, no, I did not like it. Not one little bit.

My head spun as I searched wildly for an answer.

But then, as if saved by some unseen miracle, Mrs. Spencer abruptly appeared at the top of the stairs. "Jack, your dad just pulled up in his car. It's quite late. You'd better not keep him waiting."

And gulping in relief, I watched as Jack jumped quickly to his feet; the expression of relief evident on his face as well.

After one last glance in my direction, he looked towards Millie and then her mom, thanking them both for having him and then gathered up his movies and made his way down the stairs.

Following him to the doorway, we waved goodbye as we watched the car pull away.

"He's such a nice young boy!" Mrs. Spencer exclaimed from her spot behind us.

"Yes, he is," Millie replied, as we closed the door and made our way back up the stairs.

She did not mention her Truth question again, and for that I was grateful.

But I was convinced she already knew the real answer.

The arrival…

The next few days flew quickly by and before I knew it, Saturday morning had arrived and I was sitting at home on my own, trying to find something to keep busy, anything at all to occupy myself and to stay distracted.

At the exact same time I was well aware that Millie, Jack, and Blake were all in Mrs. Spencer's car, headed towards the airport. Julia's plane would arrive in exactly one hour and they had left early in order to find a car park and to be there waiting when she walked through the arrival gates.

Millie had already told me the details of their surprise welcome. Julia was only expecting Millie to be at the airport with her mom and had no idea that the boys would be there as well.

I could easily picture the scene as the three friends rushed towards Julia, throwing their arms around her in a huge welcoming hug. And I could also imagine the reunion between her and Blake, who according to Millie, was the love of Julia's life.

Sighing to myself, I moped around the house…the memory of Millie's promise ringing in my ears.

"Emmie, you'll have to come over to my house so you can meet Julia. I'll find out what's happening with rehearsals and then I'll text you. Hopefully, we can arrange a time for Monday. Unless you have something else planned?"

"No, that sounds great, Millie," I had replied, knowing full well that I would not be busy. I had no plans whatsoever.

My mom didn't usually work on weekends but that morning she had a ton of paperwork to catch up on, so I waited impatiently for her to finish so we could head out together and do something. Anything to take my mind off what I could not stop thinking about.

With nothing else to do, I spent the morning looking at YouTube videos and checking out online shopping websites. These were something that Millie had introduced me to and although I'd already spent the clothing allowance my mom had given me, it was fun to look anyway. And besides that, it helped to pass the time.

After a while, I decided to check my Instagram feed, knowing full well that Millie would be sure to post a photo of Julia once she'd arrived. And sure enough, it popped up instantly; a picture of a really pretty girl with long brown hair and beautiful big eyes. She was wearing a gorgeous green skirt and a black and white crop top. Millie stood alongside her and the pair had their arms wrapped around each other in a welcoming hug. It was such a great pic and clearly showed how happy they were to be together again.

But it was the post underneath that tore at my heart the most…

Amazing to be with my best friend again! Welcome back, Julia! I've missed you so much!

@juliajones

With another deep sigh, I tossed my phone down onto the bed and reached for my teddy. Right then, I just needed a hug. He was always there for me and hugging him always helped.

But that morning as I clutched him tightly to my chest, I could feel the tears drip slowly down my cheeks. I knew I was being silly. I knew I was being childish and I knew I was being selfish. They had every right to enjoy their time together. And I had no right to complain.

But right then I didn't care.

Completely still, I sat quietly in that very spot and remained there without moving until I heard my mom's voice calling me into the kitchen for lunch.

Dread…

Finally, Monday arrived and as promised, Millie's text appeared on my phone but it was not what I'd been hoping for.

So sorry Emmie, can we hang out another day this week? Julia and I are so busy with stuff that we won't have any spare time today. But she is dying to meet you! Talk soon! Xxx

Hugely disappointed, I did not want to stay in the house with nothing to do. So I asked for permission to head into the mall and made plans to meet my mom later for lunch.

I'd browsed the shops in that mall so many times, that I knew them back to front. Luckily though, the paved area was bustling with a variety of street entertainers, some of whom I'd seen before but also a couple of new ones.

The sweet sound of a girl singing and playing guitar caught my attention and I headed in the direction of her voice. I could see that a huge crowd had gathered and I wondered absently if she was also planning to enter Carindale's Got Talent.

As I moved closer and found a spot amongst the crowd where I was able to get a better view, I realized with a surprised gasp that Millie and Jack were standing amongst the audience on the opposite side of the circle. And when I took a closer look, I caught sight of a really pretty girl alongside them.

When I watched Millie turn towards her with a smile,

obviously commenting on the singer, I saw the girl next to her smile in return, her beautiful features lighting her face.

So that was Julia. I could clearly see in that instant, that she was even prettier than in her photographs.

A boy who I assumed was Blake stood behind her; all four were captivated by the singing of the girl, whose amazing voice was attracting loud applause from the entire crowd.

While I pretended to watch the girl's performance, my focus was on the group of friends on the other side. I could not take my eyes from them.

As I stood there, I began to sense the familiar prickle of discomfort on the back of my neck and I froze in my place; the sight of Millie, Jack and the others standing amongst the crowd on the other side, momentarily forgotten.

Not daring to turn around, I kept my focus ahead, feeling sure that the mysterious, creep of a man had found me yet again.

But then, unable to stand still and do nothing, I slowly scanned the area behind me, expecting to see his glaring eyes on mine at any moment. Surprisingly, however, he was nowhere to be seen.

The prickling sensation continued, and feeling alert and afraid, I looked around once more. That was when I noticed a boy around my age standing nearby. What caught my attention was his intense gaze as he stared directly across the circle. However, his eyes were not on the singer, but instead, he looked directly towards the crowd on the other side.

He had no idea that I'd noticed him but I could feel the hatred dripping from his evil scowl. Pushing through to the thoughts in his head, I gasped with shock, the words I was hearing filling me with dread.

"Julia Jones! What are you doing back in town? And you're still hanging out with that loser! Do you seriously think I'm going to let you get away with what you did? I haven't forgotten. And your time will come."

My mouth agape, I stood motionless and in shock. What was going on? Why did he hate Julia so much? And who was the person he was referring to? He was calling one of them a loser and I had no idea who. What I was completely sure of though was that he'd meant every word he had said.

Then, as he turned abruptly around and moved away from the crowd, I watched him disappear down the length of the mall; all the while his intense hatred lingering in the air.

With a sickly feeling, I looked again towards the group opposite.

And taking a deep breath, I tried to calm my racing pulse.

Book 2

It's Complicated!

Unsure...

I had a bad feeling about the strange boy in the mall that day. When I caught sight of him staring across the crowd towards Millie and the others, as they watched the performance of a super talented singer, I knew immediately that something was not quite right.

With his thoughts filtering through to my own, I became aware of the frightening words being spoken in his head. While he was not a threat to me, I knew instantly that he was definitely a concern for Julia. He appeared to be planning revenge and although I had no idea of the reason, his intentions were very clear.

He wanted Julia and her "loser" friend to pay for what they'd done. They were his exact words and although I had no idea what incident he was referring to, he was obviously quite determined to go ahead with his plan. A dripping hatred poured from his intense stare, which was both ugly and frightening at the same time. It made my skin crawl.

Pleased to see him eventually turn away, I stood watching as he disappeared into the crowd of shoppers who filled the mall and hoped that I'd been mistaken. Perhaps I'd misinterpreted his thoughts and there was nothing to worry about after all.

But I struggled to believe that was the case, and worse still, I knew there was very little I could do about it.

There was no way I could bring myself to walk up to Julia and warn her. I knew who she was but we hadn't even been introduced yet and I could just imagine how weird she'd think I was if I tried to explain.

"Hey, Julia. I'm Millie's new friend, Emmie. I just read this kid's mind and I don't want to scare you but he was making a terrible threat. I think you might be in danger."

As if I could really say that! She'd probably think I was crazy and simply laugh it off. She'd probably also wonder why Millie had become friends with someone so odd.

As well as wanting to avoid that scenario completely, if I gave away my secret it would be sure to land me in all kinds of trouble. I'd tried that before and knew from experience what the result would be. Plus, I'd promised my mom and also myself that I would keep my mouth shut.

Carindale was a fresh start for us both and I did not want to be the cause of us having to move again; especially not after becoming friends with Millie and then meeting her friend, Jack, the boy who I had not stopped thinking about.

There was definitely too much at stake. So I just had to hope that the hateful boy in the mall would change his mind and not follow through with his silent threat after all.

Deciding that I needed to put it all behind me and forget what I had heard, I turned back towards the singer. But when I searched the crowd for Millie and the others, I found that they were nowhere in sight. With the area full of people, it was clear that they could have gone in any direction and I had missed my opportunity to join them.

When I'd first spotted the group of friends, it had taken me by complete surprise and I was too shy to even consider the idea of heading over towards them. I knew that only a short time earlier, they had collected Julia from the airport and I did not want to intrude on their time together, especially as Julia had just arrived. As the minutes ticked past though, I worked up the courage to go and say hello. But then I became distracted and in that time they had disappeared. So I was forced to remain standing on my own.

Meanwhile, the young girl singing continued to entertain the crowd with her amazing voice and for a moment, I compared her talent with Millie's. If they were to compete against each other, I felt sure it would be a close competition. Although the girl was several years older, Millie's voice was almost as good, but then, perhaps I was biased and I wondered what a panel of judges would think.

I guessed we would all soon find out because Carindale's Got Talent was not too far away. This thought reminded me of the time that Millie would need to spend with the others if they were going to be ready to perform.

Naturally, they would need lots of ongoing practice that would take up a lot of her spare time…time that I could be spending hanging out with Millie if she were not involved. Thinking once more of Millie's promise to contact me, I recalled her words.

"I'll text you early next week, Emmie," she had said. "I can't wait for you to meet Julia. I've told her all about you!"

While I was sure that she would follow through on that promise and I really was looking forward to finally meeting Julia, at the same time I felt quite nervous about it all. There had been such a big build up and although I was sure that I'd like her, I was worried that she might not like me.

What if she thought I was weird or strange, like so many other people who I'd met in the past? And worse still, what if she wanted to keep Millie to herself? That was my biggest fear and try as I might, I could not push that thought away.

It had been shaping up to be such a fun summer and then Julia had unexpectedly arrived and all my plans had changed.

As soon as I'd spotted the group amongst the crowd, it was instantly obvious how close they all were.

During the few minutes that I watched them, they had not stopped chatting and laughing, and the entire time Blake had not taken his eyes off Julia. I could see first-hand that Millie had not been exaggerating when she told me how close the two were and I considered once again, how hard it must have been for Julia to move away.

Jack had also caught my attention and although I tried to keep my feelings in check, I could not help but notice his cheeky grin, the one that continued to captivate me each time I saw him. His outgoing and funny personality made it impossible not to like him and I understood why Millie had regained her old crush. I'd come to terms with that fact though and did not want to interfere or come between them. Jack was Millie's crush and I had to accept that.

They were such a great group of friends and I was hoping more than anything to become a part of that group. But if I wanted that to happen I knew I needed to be positive and stay patient. That was what I had to focus on, rather than the opposite. If I did that I was sure Millie would remain true to her word and text me as promised.

Then quite surprisingly, the much-anticipated text arrived even sooner than I had expected.

The next day...

Groggy and half asleep, I reached towards the little table beside my bed grasping clumsily for my phone. I had barely heard the sound of the text alert and had almost chosen to ignore it. After a late night the evening before where my mom and I spent several hours watching a Harry Potter marathon on television, I had planned to sleep in and was not at all interested in being disturbed. But then the phone made another vibrating, bleeping sound and that one actually managed to register in my tired brain.

Sitting bolt upright, I keyed in my passcode so I could access the message. Apart from my mom, the only person I received texts from was Millie and the realization that it was, in fact, her name on the screen was enough to bring my senses quickly into focus.

Hey, Emmie! Are you free today?

With an eager smile, I typed my reply.

I don't have any plans at all. What are you up to?

Waiting patiently for her return message, I felt the smile spread wide on my face.

Overjoyed that it was only Julia's second day in town and I was already being invited to hang out with them, I grinned excitedly.

It's a beautiful day and Julia and I thought we'd go to Wet 'n Wild, It's a really cool water park in Carindale. You'll love it!

Processing the words in front of me, I felt the joy that had just been bubbling inside melt rapidly away.

I'd heard about the water park that Millie was talking about and I was sure it would be heaps of fun. But the problem was that it involved swimming! I could not believe that of all possible options they had chosen the one thing I always tried my hardest to avoid!

With a huge sigh, I glanced out the window and took in the rays of warm sunshine that poured through the glass and onto my bed. The blue sky beyond was vivid and inviting and it was obviously a perfect day, so I could understand the reason for their choice.

The issue for me was the memory of my past experiences and pangs of unease fluttered in my stomach. It had been quite some time since I last went swimming but I clearly remembered the silent remarks from the other kids about the skinny girl they were all staring at.

Although what they were saying in their heads was true, it was the mean words they were using that hurt so much.

I knew exactly what they were thinking and their hurtful comments were still fresh in my mind and still just as upsetting as the day I'd heard them.

Alerted by the sound of another text, I realized that I hadn't replied and that Millie was waiting impatiently for an answer. From what I could see, I had two choices. I could make up an excuse and say no, then spend the day at home moping around the house and feeling sorry for myself. Or, I could go along and more than likely have a great day.

Millie and Julia wanted to hang out with me and I knew I should be grateful that Millie had contacted me so quickly. Although it was totally unexpected and had come as a complete surprise, it would be awfully dumb to say no. After all, it was what I'd been hoping for.

I was also aware of the fact that it had been a couple of years since I'd last worn a swimsuit in public and while I still felt that my body shape was too thin, perhaps my mom was right and I had begun to look a little better. After all, Millie had even commented on how much she envied my figure.

Making a quick decision, I took a deep breath and began to type.

Sounds great! What time are you planning to go?

A moment later I reread my text, hesitating before hitting Send.

But a sudden pang of determination, and a growing excitement about the day ahead helped me to make up my mind. Not stopping to hesitate for another second, I hit the Send key and jumped quickly out of bed.

Remembering the pretty sky-blue swimsuit that my mom

had bought on sale, just a couple of weeks earlier, I pulled open my cupboard drawers in search of them. Not sure where I'd stashed them though, they took some time for me to find.

At the time, I'd hidden them away, convinced that I'd probably never wear them. But as they were my favorite color and the latest style, Mom had been hoping that I would change my mind. Up until that day, I'd had no desire whatsoever to do that.

After abruptly changing my mind and deciding I'd be brave enough to put them on, after all, I prayed that I no longer looked as skinny in swimmers as I once had. I knew there was only one way to find out though and that was to try them on and hope for the best.

But just as I pulled the new swimsuit with the tags still fully attached from the bottom of my cupboard drawer, I heard the bleep of yet another message.

And this one made me more nervous than ever!

Unexpected…

When Millie's car pulled up in my driveway a short time later, I headed anxiously out the front door. Her earlier text had explained that she'd asked her mom to pick me up and would soon be on her way. This had come as a surprise and I was forced to hurry so I'd be ready when they arrived. But what made the situation so much more intense was the fact that she had also asked Jack and Blake to join us.

It had been one thing to meet Julia, but to have the two boys come along as well was not what I'd been expecting. Although I had imagined that very scenario so many times, the realization that I was spontaneously being faced with that reality, had become quite nerve-wracking; especially as I'd been dreaming of it happening for so long.

Nervous and unsure, I made my way down the driveway, glad that my mom was in tow. She wanted to say hello to Millie's mom as well as meet the two boys I'd been talking about.

Grateful for her friendly, talkative nature, I stood quietly by her side as we were all introduced.

Her outgoing manner helped me to overcome the shyness that I was feeling.

My mom is such a chatterbox!!

I soon discovered I had absolutely nothing to worry about. Julia's beaming smile and warm greeting instantly put me at ease and I could tell immediately that she was every bit as nice as Millie had promised. I did not attempt to read her thoughts at all, as I felt so comfortable in her presence that it was completely unnecessary.

"It's so great to meet you at last!" she exclaimed excitedly. "Millie hasn't stopped talking about you!"

Glancing gratefully at Millie, I hid my surprise. I had not expected Julia's comment and had certainly not expected that Millie would be talking about me! The other surprise was that Julia seemed not the slightest bit envious of that fact and it made me like her even more.

Then she turned towards Blake, who was standing quietly at her side. "Emmie, this is Blake. You haven't met him yet have you?"

When the friendly smile spread quickly across his face, I could see instantly that he was just as friendly as Julia. "Hey, Emmie. Great to meet you!"

Grinning widely, he edged just a little bit closer to Julia and it was obvious that he was very happy to be a part of the day's plans. I think that he would be happy to be anywhere Julia was. He certainly seemed pleased to have her back in Carindale.

Julia smiled at him in return. I could almost feel the magic connecting them and could see that their feelings were mutual.

Within minutes, we were all chatting as if we'd known each other for ages. It was just as I'd pictured in my mind and when the car pulled away we all waved goodbye to my mom. I felt an overwhelming happiness; all my previous worries melting quickly into oblivion.

Right then, it seemed that nothing could go wrong. It was a beautiful day, the sun was shining and I'd been given the opportunity to be a part of the group I'd been thinking about for so long.

It was certainly a morning full of surprises, ones that I had definitely not been expecting.

I soon found out, however, that the surprises would continue, although I had no idea whatsoever of the crazy situation I would later find myself a part of.

The water park...

The water park proved to be a fantastic choice. It included several different sized swimming pools, a really fun water slide, some diving boards of different levels and even a huge inflatable obstacle course that kept us entertained for hours.

Although the place ended up becoming quite crowded, it was not too much of a problem as there was so much to do. And as we had arrived early, we managed to find a great spot on an open grass area where we could sit and spread our towels for sunbathing. Not that we ended up doing too much of that because there was way too much fun to be had.

To begin with, the boys were so excited to try the diving boards that they quickly pulled off their T-shirts, dumped them on the grass alongside the rest of their gear and raced towards the water.

Meanwhile, Millie, Julia and I took our time to get ready, placing our clothes in neat piles and helping each other to apply sunscreen. Very shy in my new swimsuit at first, I stood quietly alongside them not wanting to draw attention to myself.

But when Julia turned towards me, her words gave me the confidence boost I desperately needed.

"Emmie, I absolutely love your swimsuit! Where did you get it?"

Before I had a chance to reply, Millie continued admiringly, "Emmie, I am so jealous! You look so good!"

Beaming with relief, I commented on the swimsuit that they were both wearing. At the same time though, I reached into their minds to find out if their thoughts really did match their words. While I was fairly certain that I would not find any surprises, my past experiences were too hurtful to ignore and I needed to be sure. But as I'd hoped, there was nothing at all for me to worry about.

Standing a little taller and feeling so much more confident, I made my way to the water's edge where I was abruptly hit with a splash of cold water.

Squealing in surprise, I looked into the pool to find the culprit and saw Jack grinning mischievously back. Before I had time to react, I found myself in mid-air and then quickly submerged beneath the cold water. When I came to the surface, I spotted Millie laughing alongside me. She had obviously pushed me in and was ready for more fun.

"Come on!" she cried loudly, "Let's all try the inflatable."

Following the others, I swam behind them in the direction of the massive inflatable shape that took up almost half the length of the Olympic sized pool. As I swam, I said a quiet thanks in my mind.

Extremely grateful to be a part of the fun, I realized how lucky I was. And when Jack helped to pull me up onto the edge of the pool, I could not ignore the fluttering of butterflies in my stomach.

While I did my best not to encourage him, he seemed constantly at my side, helping me through the obstacle course and grabbing hold of my hand when I slipped. Amongst squeals and shrieks of laughter from each of us, I could not help but notice him. I also noticed Millie's sideways glances.

Determined not to make things awkward, I tried to keep my distance from Jack and focus on the girls instead. But when the boys finally convinced Millie, Julia and I to try the diving boards, it was someone else who caught my attention.

In that moment, I completely forgot about Jack and his friendly behavior. At first, I had to do a double take to be sure. But when I looked a second time, I knew immediately.

The sight of this person caused a slight churn in the pit of my stomach as well as an instant chill. Although the day was hot and the water temperature had become quite mild, I still felt goose bumps appear on my skin.

What is he doing at the water park on the very same day that we also decided to come?

The question floated around in my head.

Of course, it could be coincidence, but right then, I was not so sure; especially when I noticed his familiar glaring stare. Even though we were a distance away, I knew that I'd know it anywhere.

That was when my senses went into overdrive and his silent thoughts automatically found their way into my own.

As I'd suspected his presence that day was no accident at all.

Uneasy…

Chasing after the others, I tried to ignore the apprehension I was feeling. It had been such a fun morning and I wanted nothing to spoil it. When I realized the others were headed up the ladder towards the tallest diving board, I struggled to control my unease.

"Come on Emmie," Jack called out from above. "Don't be a chicken!"

Laughing in response, I shook my head. Although I was quite a good swimmer, I was unsure of going so high and the thought in itself was making me nervous. But then I watched one kid do a perfect dive and he made it look so easy. He looked very young as well and I decided that if he could do it, surely I could too.

Keen to at least give it a try, I climbed the steps towards a lower diving board that jutted out over a different pool on the other side. It was not necessary to go all the way to the higher level and I felt that I could probably cope with the lower one.

When I reached the edge of the plank though, it seemed much higher than I had expected and I almost turned back. However, there were other kids waiting for their turn behind me so I had no choice but to continue.

Reluctant to dive from that height and risk doing a massive belly flop, which would be very embarrassing as well as very painful, my plan was to jump instead.

I could hear the others calling to me from above. They were all looking down, waiting for me to jump before they had their own turn; keen to watch and cheer me on. A lifeguard was monitoring the jumping and diving so that only one person leaped into the water at a time and also to ensure that the water was clear below. This helped to prevent a person from accidentally landing on someone else.

With nowhere to go except into the water, I squeezed my eyes tightly shut and took a flying leap.

Seconds later, I felt myself plunge into the cold depths of the pool and it took a moment for me to make my way back to the surface.

Afterwards, I realized that it hadn't been as scary as I'd imagined, and then, filled with adrenalin I decided to give the higher board a go.

I waited for the others to take their plunge and I stood by the edge of the pool so I could watch as each of them hit the water. The boys did massive bomb dives that splashed huge amounts of water out of the pool and it was a wonder they didn't empty it. The grins on their faces when they finally reached the surface again and shook the hair and water out of their eyes, clearly showed how much fun they were having. Even the shouts from the lifeguard reminding them that bomb dives were banned, didn't seem to bother them.

They quickly made their way back up the steps ready for another turn.

When I followed behind, I felt the urge to glance behind me. He was there! And only a few steps further down! Once again, I caught sight of his glaring look.

With no other option, I continued on my way but at the same time, wondered what would happen when we all reached the platform at the top.

Ignoring the uneasy feeling that had taken hold, I focused on each step in front of me, one at a time. Slippery with water, the surface underfoot caused me to slide at one point and I had to grab hold of the handrail to prevent myself from slipping over.

But keeping my eyes forward, I followed along behind the long queue of people also making their way to the top. Millie, Julia, Jack, and Blake were also making their way up the steps.

Right at that moment though, I wished they were somewhere else.

Not impressed…

When we eventually reached the top, we were forced to wait on the steps for the people in front of us to have their turn. They were all being held up by a girl who was reluctant to move from her place on the diving board. Although her friends were trying to coax her back, it appeared that she was frozen to the spot and unwilling to move in any direction.

From my spot, I could see that one of her friends had been given permission to make his way along the board to help her. Eventually, it seemed that he managed to persuade her to jump along with him. He held her hand firmly.

I was sure that her blood-curdling scream could probably be heard all over the center and we watched with fascination as she hit the water with a huge splash. When she finally reached the surface, gasping for breath, we could easily see the relief on her face. Then she quickly climbed out of the pool and left the area. I was fairly convinced that she probably wouldn't be attempting that again soon.

"That happens a lot," said the attendant as he stood on the platform directing the other kids one at a time. "People get up here and then realize they're too scared to go any further. But that girl was probably one of the worst!"

Wishing that I hadn't heard his comment, I felt my anxiety increase. And when I looked down and realized how high up we were, I instantly regretted my decision to try the high diving board.

Refusing to go first, I watched as each of my friends had their turn, one after the other. Blake, then Jack, both did skillful dives; and then Millie and Julia, both jumping feet first with a loud squeal as they fell towards the water.

Then it was my turn and I had to decide. Was I going to take the challenge or head back down the steps?

Because both Millie and Julia were brave enough, I knew that I could not back out and besides that, there was a stream of people behind me, along with the creepy person whom I wanted to avoid.

Making my way tentatively to the edge, I struggled to look down into the water. From that position, it seemed ridiculously high and I realized that it appeared much higher than it seemed from below.

Just as I moved towards the very edge, I felt the board shake quite violently beneath my feet. The strong bouncing motion caught me off guard and I looked back to see what was causing it.

Trying to keep my balance and prevent myself from slipping over, I could not turn right around but caught sight of a blurred figure racing towards me. With a shocked gasp, I felt a firm shove from behind and found myself sharply hurled into mid-air and headed for the water.

My lips were clamped together in fear and I was unable to scream. Squeezing my eyes shut, I waited for the splash of water as my feet broke the surface. But it seemed to take forever.

The cold sensation as I hit the water took my breath away and I found myself plunging towards the bottom. Down, down, down I went, unable to stop my descent.

Struggling for breath, I pushed out frantically with my arms and legs, desperate to create an upward motion in order to reach the light I could see shining above the surface.

Gasping for breath, I felt instant relief when my head finally reached the top and I was instantly reminded of the terrified girl who had been encouraged to jump, just a short time before.

In disbelief, I glanced around for the evil person who had pushed me. I knew who it was, but could see him nowhere in sight.

Then I looked up towards the diving board I had just been pushed from and spotted him standing on the edge. I couldn't understand why he would do such a crazy, stupid thing. And when I swam to the pool edge and was helped out of the water by Jack, I did not expect his response.

"Awesome jump, Emmie!"

"Didn't you see that kid push me?" I asked in surprise, wondering why he hadn't remarked on how stupid and dangerous that had been.

Shaking his head in confusion, I could see it was clear he had no idea what I was talking about.

But then I realized they'd been standing at the base of the tower and all they would have seen was my descent through the air and into the water.

And then I spotted him.

His head popped up out of the water right in front of us and when I stared angrily towards him, the creepy grin on his face turned my stomach.

"Oh, my gosh," Julia exclaimed suddenly. "What's he doing here?"

Everyone's attention was directed to the water and the boy who Julia was referring to. Disappearing under the surface and out of view, he swam beneath the water to the other side.

"Who's that?" asked Millie curiously, as she watched the figure climb out of the pool and head away towards another area.

"Ryan Hodges!" Julia stated loudly, the disgust obvious in her voice. "He was probably the only reason I was glad to leave Carindale. I can't believe he's still living here. I thought he was moving away!"

Explanation...

We sat in a group on a patch of grass, our towels spread out beneath us. The area was quite crowded at that stage with many people taking a break for lunch. As we were all starving, we were more than happy to join everyone sitting around us.

I had finally calmed down after my shocked reaction to being shoved off the end of the highest diving board I'd ever been brave enough to experience. But we were all deep in conversation over the kid whose name, according to Julia, was Ryan Hodges.

As soon as I spotted him shortly after our arrival that morning, I had recognized him immediately as the creepy kid from the mall; the one who'd been thinking the evil thoughts about Julia. Although I couldn't tell the others about all the terrible things he'd been planning, I listened intently as they explained who he was and where he had come from.

Apparently, he'd been stalking Julia for several weeks towards the end of the school year and this ended up in a full-on fistfight with Blake. This was something I found hard to comprehend especially considering Blake's kind and friendly manner. He did not seem the type of kid who would get into a fight.

It was obvious that Blake really cared about Julia though and I could imagine that he'd want to stand up for her. The idea seemed quite romantic when I thought about it and it reminded me of a knight in shining armor protecting the beautiful girl in distress. I pictured a scene where he would pull out his sword and come running to the rescue.

Smiling to myself, I watched the pair as they sat side by side on Julia's towel sharing the platter of food in front of them. They were so cute together and I tried to imagine how it would feel to have such a good-looking boy adore you the way that Blake adored Julia.

My gaze automatically fell on Jack who was hungrily biting into his burger. He must have felt me watching him because he looked my way and grinned. I could not help the familiar flutter in my stomach and quickly looked away, at the same time feeling the embarrassed blush creep over my face.

My reverie was then interrupted by Julia's hateful comments towards Ryan. I couldn't imagine her being mean to anyone but she certainly did not like that kid and I could easily understand why.

"He is the biggest creep! I still have nightmares about him stalking me!"

Her expression was one of intense dislike and I could see that the others felt the same way.

"It's so typical that he'd pull a stunt like that. Pushing a random girl off the diving board is just weird.

He's such a loser! I just hope for his sake that we don't bump into him again!"

Blake's comment caused a shiver of apprehension to run down my spine. For some reason, it made me feel quite ill about what could happen if we did see Ryan again. I also felt sure that it wasn't a random decision to shove me into the water. I was convinced that he knew I was friends with Julia and Blake and had planned it all along.

Although why he would target me, was definitely strange.

Julia's comment about him stalking her also made me worry. If he was so obsessed with her while they were still at school, had he had enough time to get over that? Or had her sudden return to Carindale brought back his obsession? I also remembered his thoughts of revenge when I'd read his mind at the mall. And I suspected that the "loser" he'd been talking about was Blake.

All the pieces of the puzzle were fitting together and the angry thoughts I'd found swirling around in Ryan's head seemed to make sense. He had not forgotten the fight or the consequences that he suffered afterward. Being expelled from school right before graduation along with the humiliation of Julia not being interested in him had been too much. And he wanted someone to pay for that.

Of course, Julia and Blake were oblivious to all of this and I was unable to warn them.

But because I'd found out what was going on, perhaps I could help to protect them. Maybe I could be their knight in shining armor and the one to help fend off evil people like Ryan.

While the thought caused me to smile, I also quite liked the idea of being a type of protector for my new friends.

We were all getting along so well and this could be my payback and a way of saying thanks for including me in their group.

With the smile returning to my face, I munched on the sandwich in my hand and when the others talked about trying out the water slide next, I immediately agreed.

There was still a lot of fun to be had but I just prayed we would not see Ryan Hodges again.

At least not that day.

And pushing thoughts of him from my mind, I concentrated on finishing my lunch so we could get back into the water.

An invitation...

During the following week, I ended up hanging out with Millie and Julia on a couple of different occasions. First of all, Millie invited me to her house one afternoon for a swim in the pool.

Her swimming pool was something I had admired on my first visit to her house and that afternoon, I was able to enjoy the beautiful setting in her backyard. It was almost like a resort and surrounded by soft green grass that made a great surface to spread our towels on for sunbathing.

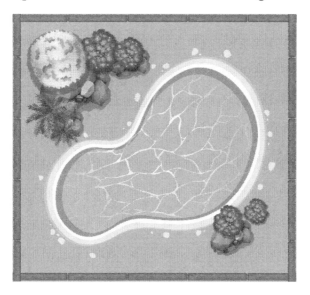

This was a great chance to spend time with just the two girls. Without Blake around, I was able to get to know Julia a lot better and she spent the afternoon telling me all about her life in the country.

I think we hit it off really well because I shared her love for horses.

Millie seemed to switch off every time Julia mentioned that topic so Julia was ecstatic to have someone to talk to about the one thing that had made her move to the country so much easier.

The subject of horses was one that I could talk about for hours and I was completely fascinated to hear about the different breeds that she'd been looking at buying. Although I'd always loved horses and had dreamed of having my own, I didn't really know too much about them. The fact that there were several different styles of riding and that it was necessary to find a horse with the right temperament and abilities to match the needs of the rider, was all new to me.

I could also see how much the idea of getting a horse had helped Julia to settle into her new home.

"Without that promise, I never would have gone," she admitted, a serious frown appearing on her face.

"Leaving the home where I've lived my entire life and all of my friends behind was the hardest thing I've ever done. I miss everyone so much, especially Millie and Blake of course. And for the first week, all I did was hide in my room and cry. I hated it!"

I looked sympathetically towards her. The emotion on her face showed how hard it had all been and I could easily understand the difficulty she faced in leaving behind such a great group of friends; especially in order to move to a random place where she knew no one at all. That would have been terrible!

"But it's awesome to be back so soon!" she continued happily, the smile returning to her lips.

"Without Millie's brainwave to enter our band into Carindale's Got Talent, this never would have happened."

The mere mention of the competition re-sparked Millie's interest in the conversation and she piped up excitedly.

"Emmie, you should come to our rehearsal on Friday! Then you can see us perform. I'm dying to hear what you think!"

"That's a great idea," Julia agreed. "It would be fun to have you there!"

"I'd love to do that!" I replied eagerly. "Oh my gosh, I can't wait to see you all play together. But are you sure it's okay for me to come?"

When they both nodded their heads in unison, and I could see their genuine enthusiasm at the idea, I was overcome with excitement. In actual fact, I found it hard to find the words to describe how I was feeling right then.

And then two days later, true to her promise, Millie's car pulled up in my driveway once again. This time it was only Millie and Julia in the back seat but as was the case the time before, both girls were smiling happily about having me join them.

And for about the tenth time in only a few days, I wondered if my life could get any better!

The rehearsal...

The afternoon was even more fun than I had anticipated. And Millie's band was better than I could have possibly imagined.

At first, I felt a little awkward, as the boys were quite surprised to see me there. They had obviously not been expecting me and I felt like an intruder, invading their space. I muttered a quick explanation about wanting to see them perform and promised not to get in the way. Then Jack, who must have sensed my embarrassment, quickly put me at ease with his cheeky grin and funny sense of humor. Unable to resist the temptation, I searched his thoughts to find out what was actually going on in his head.

This is cool. I was hoping I'd see her again soon. I hope she likes my rapping.

Those words at least made me feel welcome but I found it hard not to blush. Turning my back, I looked for a spot to sit where I'd be out of the way, although my main reason was to hide the red flush that I could feel creeping over my face. I was also trying to hide the grin that was stuck there as well.

Watching quietly from my seat on a stool in the corner, I was fascinated by the whole process. To begin with, they had to do sound checks and warm up. Meanwhile, Julia tuned her guitar, which was probably the prettiest guitar I had ever seen. When she pulled it out of its case, I looked on in envy. She had a hot pink shoulder strap that she placed over her shoulder to support the guitar while she played. This set off the pink and purple shades of the guitar itself. Along with the red trim, the bright colors made it look so cool.

The guitar was an instrument I'd always wanted to learn and my mom had mentioned a few times in the past that when she could afford it, she'd buy me one and arrange for lessons. But that was yet to happen.

When I thought about it later, I realized that Julia and I actually had a few common interests, which seemed quite a coincidence. We both loved horses, we were both interested in playing guitar and listening to music and both of us were friends with Millie.

When I considered that idea, I also realized that perhaps Millie had missed Julia so much that she'd conjured up a replacement. As weird as that sounded, I firmly believed that if you thought about something in your mind for long enough, it would suddenly appear in your life in some way or another.

I was sure that because I'd focused so intently on being a part of this cool group of friends that I had made the situation happen. Whether or not it was true, I didn't really care because it was all working out for me and that was all that mattered. And that afternoon's rehearsal was something I would always remember.

I loved music and was always downloading the latest songs off my mom's iTunes account onto my iPod.

She didn't mind too much because she liked the same music so she was happy to listen to my choices. But listening to a live band who could play as well as my friends could, was definitely something else entirely.

With all the professional gear they had set up in Blake's garage, the sound they were able to create was better than I could ever have imagined. And to see a group of kids their age performing such cool songs and sounding so good was amazing.

Blake's ability as a drummer was what I noticed first. Millie had previously told me how good he was and although I had no experience with drumming, his skill level was obvious even to a novice like me; especially for a kid his age.

Apparently, his dad was a professional musician, so I guessed that he'd inherited his father's musical genes. As for the rest of them, they'd all obviously inherited strong musical ability from somewhere as well, because Millie, Julia, and Jack were all very talented in their own way.

I already knew how good Millie's voice was but with the microphone and the instruments backing her, her singing seemed to go to the next level.

Added to that was Julia's electric guitar which sounded awesome along with Jack's catchy rap tunes. That I think was the most surprising part of all. His rap intertwined with Millie's high voice created a unique effect. Right then, I wanted to download their music so I had it available to listen to on my iPod. I was sure that if they did a live recording, they'd probably soon have a hit song.

While I had no idea of the talent amongst the other competitors in the group section of the upcoming competition, I was convinced that my friends stood a great chance of winning.

And unable to help myself, when they finished their first song, I jumped to my feet and began to applaud.

"That was amazing!!!!" I cried, clapping loudly. "Oh my gosh, you guys are incredible!"

The beaming smiles on each of their faces warmed my heart. Jack's, in particular, was the one I took special notice of, but I could see that they all appreciated my comment. It encouraged them so much that within seconds, they'd started another song.

Sitting back down in my seat to enjoy the rest of their rehearsal, I felt that it could have gone on for hours; I knew that I would have loved every minute.

As it was, my enjoyment was abruptly cut short by the sound of my phone, the ringtone cutting through the sudden silence at the end of one of their songs.

When I realized it was ringing, I grabbed my bag off the floor where I had stashed a sweater and my wallet along with a few other bits and pieces and searched amongst the various contents to find the hidden phone.

But by the time I laid my hand on it and pulled it roughly from the bag, the ringing had stopped. With a quick glance at the screen, I realized instantly that the missed call was from my mom. I also saw that she'd tried calling several times already.

My mother was the type of protective parent who always wanted to know where I was and what I was up to, but 9 attempts to call me was going a bit too far. I had promised to be home before dark and had no idea what the urgency was. Slightly annoyed at having to call her and hoping that she wasn't going to tell me to come home early, I pressed the dial key to call her back. But when I heard her voice on the other end, I knew immediately that something was wrong.

"Emmie! Where are you?"

Her tone sounded frantic and a slight anxiety began to quickly form in the pit of my stomach.

"I'm at Blake's house with Millie, Julia, and Jack. I told you I was coming here to watch them rehearse! Why? What's wrong?" My sudden concern was causing me to be quite abrupt, but I was unable to help it.

"Oh, thank goodness you're alright!" she stammered.

And then before I could respond, she blurted out some startling news. "There was a very strange man in the mall and he spoke to me. He knows about your powers, Millie. He knows!"

The words that came through the phone filled me with fear.

And whether it was intuition or something else I wasn't sure, but the distinct picture of a familiar face appeared in my mind.

It was not an image I wanted to see and I certainly did not want to hear the words that followed.

I knew exactly who she was talking about but that didn't help me at all.

In fact, it made me feel worse than ever.

Startling news...

When Millie's mother dropped me home later that afternoon, Mom was waiting impatiently in the doorway. Once we'd waved goodbye to everyone and watched the car reverse out of our driveway, Mom quickly closed the door and locked it behind her.

"Mom, what's going on?" I asked. "Please tell me exactly what happened!"

Her worried expression did not help to ease my own concerns. Ever since her phone call, I'd been fighting the sick feeling in my stomach and it had very quickly become much worse.

"After you left for Blake's house I headed into town to do some shopping," she explained in a rush. "But when I was wandering through the fruit and vegetable market an odd looking man who was browsing the fruit section happened to catch my eye. I didn't take too much notice at first but then for some reason, I felt the urge to turn around. When I did, I found him standing stock still in the middle of the aisle staring at me.

She continued on, her tone becoming more and more distraught. "It made me very uncomfortable so I moved away to another area. But he seemed to be following. When I joined the queue at the cash register, I turned around to check where he was and found him right behind me."

Pausing for a moment, I could see her trying to make sense of what had happened. The incident had obviously frightened her and she was still slightly shaken.

"It was the strangest thing, Emmie! I just wanted to pay for the things in my trolley and leave. But then he spoke and I knew straight away what he was talking about."

"What did he say?" I asked frantically, at the same time picturing the scene in my mind.

Her anxious look was making me panic. I did not have the patience for her storytelling. I just wished that for once, she'd forget all the details and get to the point.

And then in a tumble, she blurted out the words, but that was not until she'd glanced quickly around her as if to be sure that we were alone.

"He said…she's got the powers, hasn't she? Your kid…she's got the powers!"

"At first, I had no idea what he was talking about but all of a sudden, I knew. And then he turned and left."

"That's when I called you," she added quickly. "I had to make sure you were at Blake's house and that you were okay!"

Speechless, I sat frozen to the spot, the couch I was sitting on keeping me glued in place. I was secured to the chair beneath me by an invisible force, unable to move. With the feeling of nausea sinking to the depths of my stomach, for a moment I thought I might throw up. I knew exactly what was going on in her mind and it was that whirlwind of thoughts that frightened me the most.

Emmie's not safe if we stay here. We're going to have to move again. We can't stay. She's not safe. We're going to have to go.

Those were the thoughts racing around and around inside her head, over and over and over.

My mind spun and I felt a rising anger in the back of my throat. I shook my head in denial but it was no use. Those words of hers pounded in my mind and would not stop.

Unable to control myself, I broke free from the invisible bond that had been keeping me still.

Jumping to my feet, I yelled, "NO! We are NOT moving! There is NO WAY I am moving ANYWHERE!!!"

Screaming the last word louder than the rest, I was determined to get my point across, adamant that she would listen to what I had to say.

In the past that had not been the case. I'd had no choice in the matter. Instead, she had made the decisions and almost in the blink of an eye, we were constantly packing our things and getting ready to move. And this had happened time and time again. It seemed quite clear that if things were left to her, this occasion would be no different to the rest.

Unsure how to react or what to do, she sat in front of me staring silently back. I had seen her act that way before. On several occasions, she'd had the same panicked look in her eyes. The look that I had come to know so well.

It was the expression that told me our life at that point had to change. It was for my safety, she always said. That was her excuse. And just when we'd finally settled into a place that we could call home, where I had real friends, she wanted to pack up and leave. Again.

While I knew she had my best interests at heart, this constant running away had to end. I'd had enough and I was simply not going to allow it anymore. I didn't care how creepy or how scary that strange man was. I was not going to let him control our lives.

Earlier that afternoon, as soon as she described him on the phone, I had known immediately who he was.

There was no one else who fitted that description. The greasy black hair and intense dark eyes, along with the long, black coat that he seemed to live in; I knew for sure there could be no mistake. The questions were, how did he know that she was my mom? And what did he want with us?

I did not say anything at all to Millie and the others when I finally ended my mom's call. I just pretended that everything was fine. And in the meantime, I was forced to hide the turmoil racing around inside my brain.

What was going on?

How did he know that I could read minds?

Who was he and why had he confronted my mother like that?

There were so many questions that I did not know the answer to.

However, there was one thing that I was definitely sure of.

We were not moving again!

Sleepless...

I struggled to get to sleep that night. I could hear the tree branches scraping against my bedroom window and was convinced that someone was outside. Watching and waiting. Waiting for the perfect chance to snatch me away.

Three or four times, I jumped up to double check that the window was locked. But eventually, I decided I was being paranoid and climbed back into bed, pulling the covers tightly up to my chin. Even though it was a warm night, I took comfort from the feel of the soft quilt covering my body.

At one stage I was tempted to take refuge in my mom's bed, which was something I hadn't done since I was much younger. But that would have been a mistake. If she knew I was frightened, that would not help the situation at all. And it would certainly not help me to convince her that it was okay for us to stay in Carindale.

We'd already had a teary moment that evening and I did not want a repeat of that, nor did I want to repeat my earlier outburst. Although I knew that I would stand up for myself if I had to.

I was willing to do whatever it took to make sure we stayed where we were.

My mom was aware of how I felt and I'm sure that's what prompted her decision to give me Dad's letter, hoping that it would shed some light and give us the answers we so desperately needed. But unfortunately, I was left feeling more confused than ever.

It was after dinner when she called me into her room and presented me with the pretty pink box. With a couple of different compartments and a clasp to keep it secure, I was immediately curious. I had never seen it before and wondered what might be inside.

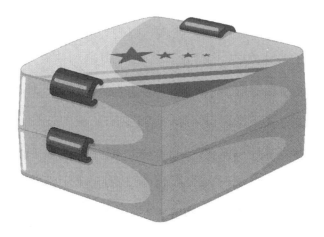

"I was saving this for your thirteenth birthday," Mom said quietly, as I took it tentatively from her. "But I think you should open it now."

Frowning slightly, I undid the clasp and lifted the lid, glancing warily inside. On the top layer was a treasure trove of mementos and keepsakes, special things that my mom had put away to remember my childhood.

As well as a lock of baby hair, there was the first tooth that I had ever lost, a plaster cast of my handprint that was made when I was four and some cute little pictures I had drawn of my family; each person drawn as an oval shape that contained a smiling face with arms and legs attached to the sides.

Mom explained each item as I pulled them out one by one. She said that it was a collection of special things she'd saved for me to show my own children one day.

I found it all quite fascinating and took my time, carefully examining each and every little thing.

At the very bottom of the box, I discovered a secret compartment. I hadn't realized it was there at first but then Mom pointed it out. And when I peeked inside, I was instantly struck by a photo of my dad's smiling face.

He was looking proudly down at the tiny baby in his arms. I had never seen that particular photo before and what caught my attention was the glow of light that seemed to shine from the two of us.

It was almost like a shimmering halo that radiated from both the man and the tiny baby that he was holding.

"That was taken just after you were born," Mom explained gently. "It's the photo that he treasured the most."

I stared at it a moment longer, and at the same time felt a tingling buzz pass through my fingertips. It was as though an electric current was connecting me to the picture and when I put it down beside me, the buzzing sensation stopped.

This abruptly reminded of a similar feeling that had passed through my body the moment my dad passed away, I pictured the moment of his death in my mind. Holding firmly to his hand at the time, the feeling had been too distinct to ignore. And flashing back to that very moment, I remembered the sensation vividly. But what seemed odd was that I should experience that exact same feeling once again.

Distracted by the one remaining item in the box, I turned towards it. The cream-colored envelope had my name neatly printed on the front and I knew instinctively that it must be a letter from my father.

On the back was a burgundy-colored stamp, shaped like a love heart.

It was just like one of those old-fashioned wax seals that were used long ago for keeping the contents of a letter secure and intact.

Staring at it curiously, I took in every detail. That was until my mom's softly spoken voice broke the silence.

"Your father wrote that letter for you about a month before he died. I promised that I'd keep it safe. He said that I would know just the right time to give it to you and I think that time is now."

Hesitant and unsure, I looked at the envelope for a moment longer, taking in every detail of the stamp that had been pressed firmly onto the back. And then, with a nod of encouragement from Mom, I carefully pried it open taking care to do as little damage to the envelope as possible.

Praying that it contained the answers I was looking for, the key to my existence and the powers I kept locked away in my head, I tried to ignore the thumping beat of my heart.

Inside there appeared to be a folded note. When I pulled it out, I found a single page of text written in black ink. As I scanned the words in front of me, I felt sure that I could hear my dad's voice inside my head, as if he were there right by my side, reading the letter to me.

To my darling Emily

When you finally get the chance to read this letter I am sure you will have grown into a beautiful young girl. My only regret is that I cannot be the one to tell you how much you have always been loved.

From the moment you were born, I knew instantly that you were special. When I held you in my arms, the light shone from your eyes and the magic surrounded you.

You are a chosen one, Emily…you are truly, truly blessed. You have been given a gift and you must treasure that gift with your heart.

Others will cross your path who also share this gift or who want to capture it for themselves. But some will seek to use it for evil and must be avoided at all costs. Use your powers wisely and in return, you will stay safe. At times you may be afraid, but the challenge will lie in staying strong. This may not make much sense at first, but I promise that in time, it will.

Just remember that I am always with you.

All my love,

Dad xxx

Handing the letter to my mother to read, I sat staring at her, hoping that she could explain.

"Mom, he was a mind reader! He had the same powers as me! But why didn't he tell you? And what does his letter mean?"

Frustrated and annoyed, I sighed deeply. Even after reading the letter through once again, I felt more bewildered than ever. Rather than answering my questions, all the note had done was confuse me. It hadn't helped at all.

And that was what had kept me awake, tossing and turning until the early hours of the morning. At the time, I didn't think that I would sleep at all.

My mom had been no help. Her thoughts were even more jumbled than my own. She was also struggling to come to terms with the secret my dad had kept from her for so long.

He said that in time his letter would make sense. While I desperately hoped that would be the case, so far all it had done was to make the situation worse.

Picturing his smiling face once more, I tried to come to terms with the simple fact that my dad had been a mind reader as well.

That was the biggest shock of all.

An idea...

I woke the following day with a terrible flu. It seemed to have come from nowhere. From the moment I'd woken, I had a very sore throat and within no time, my nose seemed to be dripping like a tap.

Symptoms such as those were always hard to cope with but in the scorching heat of summer, they were even harder to manage, especially because that day, in particular, was extremely hot. The weatherman on television had announced the evening before that we would be experiencing a heat wave during the next couple of days. Well, for once his forecast had been deadly accurate. And I was forced to wander around the house feeling miserable and sorry for myself.

What made matters worse was the text I received from Millie inviting me over for a swim.

It's so hot today! We're going to spend the afternoon in the pool. You should come over!

Unfortunately, though, even that invitation from Millie was not enough to improve the way I was feeling.

After texting back with a couple of sad emoticons attached, to describe how upset I was to be missing out on the fun, I grabbed another box of tissues from the bathroom cupboard and returned back to my spot in front of the computer.

With nothing else to do, I passed the time searching the Internet for any information I could find about mind reading. This search was one I'd conducted several times before, but that had been some time ago. Because I had never found anything useful, I'd given up looking. But after finding my dad's letter I decided on one last attempt at trying to find answers online.

As it turned out, my search proved to be much more successful than in the past. It seemed that since my previous effort, more research had been done and the result was a lengthy list of websites that I'd never come across before. Some were scientifically based and they were the ones that kept me most interested.

In fact, there was so much new information on the subject that it kept me occupied for hours.

While some sites included stories of people's experiences, most of which I found hard to believe, there were others that gave tips and instructions demonstrating how to actually become a mind reader.

It was quite fascinating to read and I wondered if anyone had ever been successful.

Although I found nothing that explained why some people were born with the skill already intact and there was no evidence to suggest that others like my dad and myself really existed, I had been hit with an idea that continued to nag at my thoughts.

According to the information I'd found, mind reading was apparently something that could be learned and for the remainder of the day, I was unable to think of anything else.

After continually tossing the idea around and around in my head, I eventually came to the conclusion that it might even work. Convincing myself that as long as I kept my own abilities secret, I decided that there was definitely no harm in trying. And at the very least, it would be an interesting experiment.

After all, what if it worked and I was able to teach someone else to read minds too?

It seemed to me that I had absolutely nothing to lose.

Reaching for another tissue, I blew loudly on my nose. Although my cold hadn't really eased at all, I felt better inside. The gut-wrenching nausea that had gripped my stomach ever since my mom's phone call the day before, seemed to have gently eased away.

Glancing at the photo from the pink box, which I had stuck inside a photo frame I'd found in my cupboard and then placed on my desk, I smiled for the first time that day.

My dad smiled back at me and I decided that everything was going to be okay.

All I had to do was listen to my intuition, which I felt sure was really my dad's voice inside my head. He was there to help me every step of the way; all I had to do was take notice. If something didn't feel right, then it probably wasn't, but right then, everything had started to feel good.

Shutting down my computer, I grabbed my phone and headed out to the kitchen. I had not been interested in my mom's earlier offer of food, but my appetite seemed to have returned. Ravenously hungry, I searched through the fridge for something to eat.

Just as I reached for the sandwich she had made for me earlier and covered in plastic wrap, I heard the beeping sound of a text on my phone.

Turning towards it, expecting to see that Millie's name had appeared on the screen, I was surprised to see that the text was not from her at all.

In fact, the name in front of me was one I had certainly not been expecting!

And unable to prevent the large grin that was quickly spreading across my face, I typed my reply.

A visitor...

When I answered the doorbell the following morning, I tried my best to control my reaction. My mom often had new clients come to the house to discuss her online business services and how she could help them with their websites, so it was certainly nothing new. What caught me by complete surprise that morning was the sight of Jack standing alongside his mother and I attempted to hide the look of shock that was plastered all over my face.

Attacked by a sudden bundle of nerves, I stammered hello to the two people staring back at me. Jack's cheeky grin certainly didn't help and when I read his mind, I knew instantly that he had planned the visit all along.

Slightly embarrassed that I looked such a mess, I opened the door and invited them both in, thankful that my mother had appeared behind me and could save me from further awkwardness.

She was always looking for new clients and had been more than happy to hear that Jack's mother needed help with her website. That was my mom's specialty and one of the main services that her online business offered. However, I had not realized when I received Jack's text the day before that he was intending to come along too.

Glancing down at my shabby old shorts and worn out T-shirt, I wished that I'd chosen something else to wear that day. But judging by the grin on Jack's face, he hadn't even noticed. Either that or he didn't care about the old clothes that I'd put on that morning. One thing I was grateful for was that at least my flu had improved and I was no longer constantly reaching for a tissue.

We followed my mother through to the kitchen, where she poured cold drinks into a glass for each of us. Jack and I sat quietly by and listened to our mothers' conversation, or should I say *my* mother's conversation. As usual, she had not stopped talking and I was waiting for her to take a breath so Jack's mom would have a chance to speak.

Rolling my eyes at Jack, I briefly shook my head and grinned. When I read his thoughts I found that he had picked up on my meaning and was chuckling to himself as he sat back and watched the scene in front of him. At least my mother's continual chatter helped to put everyone at ease, in particular, myself. That was until she invited Jack's mom into her office to discuss the work she needed to have done, and I found that Jack and I had suddenly been left in the kitchen on our own.

Still coming to terms with the realization that he had turned up unexpectedly at my front door and was sitting on a stool in front of me, I quickly created a mental wall in my mind. I was well aware that I would not be able to properly relax around him until I had blocked his thoughts and was no longer able to read his mind.

Knowing every word that was silently making its way through his head, was too distracting for me; especially when his thoughts were focused on the fact that he was very happy to be there right then. That was doing nothing at all to calm my nerves. But if I were to be completely truthful, I'd have to admit that deep down I was pleased with what I'd discovered and also that I felt exactly the same way.

Within minutes, his easy-going manner was all that was needed and the two of us were chatting and laughing, the way we always seemed to do whenever we had the chance to hang out together. Although the difference right then was that we happened to be on our own, with Millie, Julia, and Blake nowhere in sight.

In the past, Millie's bubbly presence amongst her friends had been my safety net and her outgoing personality had made me feel completely at ease whenever we were all together. But that morning, the atmosphere between Jack and I felt more comfortable than ever. So much so that after a short while, it felt completely natural to ask the question that had been in the back of my mind since I'd thought of it the day before.

The idea was something I'd been wondering about ever since, but the main dilemma had been who to try it out on. And just then, it seemed that I had the answer sitting on a stool right in front of me.

Lightbulbs...

"Jack, do you think it's possible to read minds?"

Once the words were out, I could not believe I'd said them. And blinking anxiously, I waited for his response.

"I don't know," he replied, thoughtfully. "But it would be such a cool thing to be able to do."

Perhaps it was simply because he was so easy to talk to. Or perhaps it was that after overcoming my initial shock at seeing him on my doorstep, I'd begun to feel very comfortable around him and he was the perfect person to trial my idea. I was not completely sure of the reason, but something seemed to spur me on and although I knew I had to be careful, I decided to continue.

"Well, according to these websites I've found, there are people who have learned to read minds."

"Really?" he asked, his curiosity building.

But after giving it more thought, he added doubtfully, "That's probably fake though.

There's probably a trick they're hiding."

"Yeah," I agreed, "That's what I thought at first, but then I found some other websites with instructions explaining everything. And I thought it would be cool to find out if it can really be done."

The idea had taken momentum in my head and the more I discussed it with him, the more I was convinced that he was the perfect person. Added to that was my desperate need to find someone like me.

Or at least, someone who could learn to do what came so easily to me; someone who could develop the "gift" as well. Even if it was of their own making.

Up until the day before, I had no idea if another mind reader even existed. And not only had I discovered that my dad could read minds but he had admitted in his letter that there definitely were such people, both good and bad.

I felt sure that the mysterious man from the mall was one of the evil ones my dad was referring to. And this made it even more important for me to have an ally, someone who was a friend and could help me.

Who better than Jack to fill that role? He was a perfect choice. All I had to do was help him learn. And because I was already a master, wasn't I the perfect one to teach him?

All of a sudden, everything seemed to make sense and just like light bulbs being flicked quickly on and off, the ideas and thoughts flashed through my brain.

They only stayed a moment but it was all that was necessary for me to process a plan. Becoming more excited by the minute, I grabbed Jack by the hand and asked him to follow me through to my room where my computer sat waiting.

With the realization that the websites containing the information were all there, I knew we just had to follow the instructions. My hopes were rapidly racing to the surface as I reached for the mouse. And with a quick grin in Jack's direction, I caught sight of his own mounting curiosity and excitement.

Could this be the answer I'd been looking for?

Lesson time...

"Close your eyes and take a deep breath," I instructed quietly, trying to calm my own racing pulse.

"It's kind of like meditating," I explained. "You have to breathe deeply and try to clear your mind of all thoughts. Empty it out so that you are totally relaxed and there's nothing going on inside your head."

I watched as his breathing deepened. In. Out. In. Out. Slow and steady, the rhythm continued one breath after another. I allowed him to continue until I could see him visibly relax. It was obvious by the slump of his shoulders and his relaxed posture, as well as the way in which he was no longer sitting stiffly in the chair, that he had become calm.

"Now, open your eyes," I instructed, maintaining a quiet, steady tone. "Look at me and focus. Block out all thoughts and just really focus on me. Don't think about anything else."

A wide grin appeared on his face. "That's easy!" he laughed.

Laughing in return, I shook my head. "You have to stay serious," I reminded him, even though I was unable to help my own grin. "If you're not seriously focused, then it won't work! Just look at me and try to take in the energy around me."

I took a deep breath and he mimicked my actions, gradually returning to a slow breathing pattern while staring directly at me. But I could see that he was struggling to keep a straight face. This was something I had difficulty with as well. And within seconds we were both laughing once more.

"I can't do it," he said. "It's too hard."

"That was my fault," I replied, "I lost concentration too. Let's try again."

Nodding in agreement, he returned to the steady breathing that he had been working on and I soon heard the same deep rhythmic breaths continue. In. Out. In. Out.

With his eyes focused on mine, I stared quietly back. If it was going to work, he needed help from me. Focusing my energy towards him, I tried to project my thoughts his way.

After about 30 seconds, I formed a thought in my mind. It was not at all intentional, just something that had appeared in my head.

And a single moment later, I watched him open his mouth to speak.

"This is a really cool thing to try, I'm glad you asked me to have a go!"

"That's what I was just thinking," I replied, the surprise evident in my voice.

With a pleased smile and a nod of his head in recognition, he focused again on his breathing, but at the same time, I wondered if I had read his mind before he spoke, or had he actually read mine?

Although it was most likely myself picking up on his thoughts, even with my mental wall intact, I felt sure it was a great start. What impressed me most was his willingness to take part. Most people would probably think the whole process too weird and not even be bothered to try.

Before his unexpected arrival that morning, I'd considered asking Millie, but I had my doubts as to what her reaction would be. Instead though, Jack had turned up and as usual, the timing was perfect.

While his chance arrival right then could have been coincidence, I preferred to think that it had happened for a reason. And that it was meant to be.

But regardless of whether or not it would work, I was glad to have him as my friend. He seemed to understand me in a way that no one ever had before; not even Millie. And as I continued to stare in his direction, I took in every feature on his handsome face. That was enough to shift my focus entirely and this seemed to affect his concentration as well.

Grinning widely at me, he began to laugh. "Maybe we can try this another time," he suggested, the smile still stuck to his face. "If we keep practicing, you never know what might happen."

Chuckling in agreement, I replied, "I was just thinking exactly the same thing!"

"Wow," he beamed. "That's so cool. We could be onto something!"

"Yes," I responded, happily. "We definitely could be!"

A Surprise...

When Jack and I headed into the kitchen for something to eat, we found Jack's mom sitting on a stool at the kitchen bench chatting away to my mother who was busy preparing a pot of tea.

After offering Jack some cookies, I poured Jack a cold drink and then we sat down to join them. It seemed quite clear that our mothers were getting on extremely well. I could also see that Mrs. Hillman was particularly pleased with all the services Mom could provide to help improve her website.

While this was great for my mother's business, I also realized that it would create a kind of connection for both Jack and I as well, and it was this that sparked my interest most.

Then when Mom asked Mrs. Hillman to put all her files, images and graphics onto a portable USB and drop it over so she could start work, Jack's response caught everyone's attention.

"I'm not doing anything tomorrow," he said helpfully. "I can bring it around if you want."

All pairs of eyes darted in his direction, including my own, and I immediately noticed the look of surprise on my mom's face. When I saw her slightly raised eyebrows as she glanced questioningly towards me, I knew of course what she was thinking. Choosing to ignore her reaction, I smiled at Jack, and at the same time, tried to control the dancing butterflies in my stomach.

When we later waved goodbye from our front door and watched as Mrs. Hillman's car reversed down our driveway, Mom commented with a curious glance my way. "Jack seems like a nice boy, Emmie."

Wanting to avoid each of the questions that I knew she was desperate to ask me, I quickly agreed with her comment and then headed to my room, the grin spreading across my face.

"Yes, he is a very nice boy!" I whispered quietly to myself as I closed my bedroom door behind me.

And the image of his cheeky grin flashed through my thoughts along with the excited anticipation of seeing him again the following day.

But then I pictured Millie and my smile quickly vanished.

"We're just friends, I hastily reminded myself. "Surely there's no harm in that!"

Lesson Two...

When I opened the door for Jack the next morning, I was prepared. Although I didn't want to appear too obvious, I did make sure that I was at least wearing a pretty top and some nice shorts. They weren't my favorite ones but they were much better than what I had on the day before. Also, I'd taken the time to braid my hair, which was something I'd been practicing for a while. That skill was one that had taken me some time to master and I was in awe of girls who could easily braid their own hair, with the ability to create beautiful styles that required hardly any effort at all. I may be able to read minds, but braiding hair was definitely not a skill that came naturally, not for me anyway.

Regardless of my braids and the clothes I'd chosen to wear, when I saw Jack's smiling face staring back, as usual, I had to control my racing pulse. Attacked by a churning stomach and an awkwardness that I struggled to push aside, I took a moment to wonder why he always had such an effect on me.

Forcing myself to get a grip on my emotions, I invited him inside.

But we were unable to avoid my mom who was waiting in the kitchen with a batch of freshly baked cookies and her standard one hundred and one questions. While I knew she was being her usual friendly self, I was sure she also had an ulterior motive and was interested in learning as much about Jack as she could. As well, she probably guessed that she would not be hearing too many details from me, so the only way she'd find out would be to ask him herself...

"What have you been up to these holidays, Jack?"

"I hear you're a rap singer! How did you get into that?"

"Do you play any musical instruments?"

"How's the band going?"

"What else do you like to do apart from singing rap?"

"Do you have any plans for the rest of the holidays?"

On and on and on, her questions continued and I was so scared she'd ask the most embarrassing one of all. I knew it was on her mind and the entire time, I prayed that she would keep it to herself...

"Why are you so interested in my daughter all of a sudden?"

OMG! I shuddered at the thought! But thankfully, she didn't mention that question at all and eventually, we were able to escape with Jack fairly unscathed. Although in reality, he hadn't seemed to mind too much; either that, or he was grateful for an opportunity to sit and eat more cookies. Because I must admit, my mother's baking was definitely master chef standard. And it was quite obvious by the empty plate that had been wiped spotlessly clean, crumbs and all, that Jack had certainly enjoyed her cooking.

Desperate to continue on with where we'd left off the day before, I could hardly wait to drag him to a quiet place in the living room. I was sure that if I could train him to read minds, my life would become so much better.

To have a good friend who I could share my innermost fears and feelings with and in particular, to be able to open up to another mind reader who really understood what it was like to have that ability, would be something I'd always dreamed of.

I think that issue was what bothered me the most. Rather than the obvious fact that I could read minds, it was the need for absolute secrecy that I found more difficult than anything else.

However, when Jack sat down and attempted once again to follow the instructions we'd discussed the day before, we did not get the results I was hoping for.

When I thought about it later, I realized that if it was possible to teach someone to read minds, it would require intense focus and concentration, as well as a great deal of patience.

As far as Jack and I were concerned though, neither of us was capable of that. To sit quietly focused on each other and remove all other thoughts from our heads entirely seemed an impossible task.

Either he'd start laughing, or he'd break the silence with some sort of silly comment. And if it wasn't Jack interfering with the energy flow, it was me. As well as that, the idea of sitting alone in a room with him while he stared quietly back at me was too difficult for either of us to manage.

Strangely enough, rather than being disappointed, I felt happier than ever.

To begin with, I don't remember ever laughing so much. At one stage, my mom came in to find out what all the commotion was about.

"What's so funny?" she asked, unable to hide the smile on her own face. "You two sound like you're having way too much fun!"

But her comment just caused more fits of laughter with neither of us being able to speak. And shaking her head in confusion, she walked away, realizing that she'd be waiting a while for a sensible answer.

Not that I'd ever tell her what we were up to. She'd be horrified at the thought of me even considering such an idea. To her, that would be a huge risk and she'd be worried that I would end up telling Jack everything.

If I were to be honest though, I'd have to admit that the idea of sharing my secret had tempted me a couple of times already.

I had almost blurted out the details more than once. But past memories had stopped me just in time. Those memories were still too fresh in my mind and there was no way I ever wanted to risk having to move again. The thought of being forced to leave my friends behind was too scary and upsetting to even consider.

Pushing that idea aside, I paused to glance more seriously at Jack, who was still grinning cheekily back at me. Curious to know what was going on in his head, I felt my mental wall begin to crumble and flashes of his thoughts made their way into my own.

With an embarrassed flush, I quickly rebuilt my mental barrier.

Invading his privacy that way was not the right thing to do and besides that, his thoughts were making the butterflies in my stomach go a little too crazy. I also knew that it was really not necessary to read his mind to be aware of what he was thinking. It was as though a connection had developed between us and we had tuned into the same wavelength and the same frequency.

Instantly I knew that I had finally found the friend I'd been hoping for. Millie was still my best friend, but my friendship with Jack was something different and special. Not only was he fun to be around, we just seemed to click.

Finally, comfortable in each other's presence there seemed nothing to prove. And I had the distinct feeling that if I ever told anyone what I was capable of, he would be the person I'd open up to. I also knew that he would understand.

Alerted by the loud sound of my phone's distinct ring tone, our moment of comfortable silence was broken. When I spotted the caller's name on the screen, the easy, relaxed atmosphere surrounding Jack and I seemed to instantly disappear. Just like extinguishing a match, in the flicker of an instant, the glowing flame was gone.

When Jack also spotted the name on the screen, his smile quickly faded away as well.

Guilt...

"Emmie, what are you up to today? I hope you're feeling better because Julia and I have decided to go for a bike ride. Do you want to come?"

Millie's voice on the other end of the phone was warm and friendly and she was obviously keen for me to join them. I pictured her smiling face and it made me feel guiltier than ever.

Feeling ashamed, I looked towards Jack and felt a lump form in the back of my throat. I could not overcome the guilty sensation that had overwhelmed me.

She was such a great friend and it was so nice of her to include me in her plans with Julia. I was so grateful for her friendship and I would never want to betray that. But when I glanced at Jack's handsome face looking curiously towards me, I felt as though I had deceived Millie after all.

Without any further hesitation, I made a quick decision and accepted her invitation.

"That sounds like fun, Millie. I'd love to go on a bike ride. Thanks heaps for asking me!"

For some reason though, when Millie chatted on, wondering what I'd been up to that morning, I was unable to tell her. Ridden with guilt that I had been hanging out with the boy who she had a huge crush on, without her knowing, I felt instantly ashamed.

I knew I should explain, right then and there, just tell her how it had all happened...Jack's mom had needed help with her website and Jack was bored, so he decided to come over as well. There was nothing wrong with that…was there?

And today, he had simply dropped over his mom's portable USB and stayed for a bit. Surely there was no problem in that?

But with a slightly sick feeling in my stomach, I came to terms with the idea that there actually was something more. Something had happened accidentally that I'd had no control over, or so I tried to convince myself.

I was not a good friend. I did not deserve to have Millie in my life. It had been the wrong thing to do and I knew it. I also knew that as soon as I saw her, I would tell her the truth. I owed her that much and just hoped that she would understand.

Quickly ushering Jack out the door, I said a hasty goodbye and agreed vaguely to the idea of hanging out again sometime soon.

I could see the look of disappointment on his face as he put on his bike helmet and hopped on his bike. It had been laying propped against the side of our house in the front yard and it was obvious that he'd expected an invitation to join us when I told him what Millie had planned. After all, his bike was already there and when Millie and Julia arrived, we could all just cycle off together.

But the look on Millie's face if she saw him at my house was not something I wanted to imagine and I avoided the suggestion completely.

Taking a deep breath, I took comfort in the idea that I was doing the right thing in getting rid of Jack and then I could explain all the details to Millie as soon as she arrived. All the while though, I could not remove Jack's disappointed face from my thoughts and wondered briefly when I would see him again.

I just hoped that things wouldn't become awkward between us because that would be the worst feeling of all.

The bike ride ...

When I saw Millie's welcoming smile and she wrapped her arms around me in a warm hug, I felt worse than ever.

Millie, I have a crush on Jack. I know you like him but I do too. I'm sorry but I can't help it!

The words swirled frantically around in my head. But there was no way I could bring myself to utter them out loud.

So instead, I climbed on my bike and followed Millie and Julia down the driveway, promising myself that I'd mention the subject at the first available opportunity. After all, the pavement that ran along the side of that stretch of road was quite narrow and we were forced to ride in single file, so it was impossible to chat.

Even when we reached the bike path that ran through the nearby park and led along a very beautiful section of countryside towards the outskirts of town, there was still not enough space for the three of us to ride side by side. So, I was forced to wait, and as the trees and bushes whizzed by, so did my resolve to own up to the truth.

And when we finally stopped for a rest, another bike rider appeared off the track behind us and all my thoughts of Jack disappeared completely.

The grassy section of the park that contained a playground and a water fountain had looked like the ideal spot to rest…I was desperate for a drink. I was annoyed that I'd forgotten to bring a water bottle, which seemed such an obvious thing to have remembered.

Although my flu had improved dramatically, I was still not one hundred percent and was also beginning to feel quite tired.

Grateful for the chance to stop, I questioned my decision to agree to the ride after all.

But when the cyclist behind us decided on a similar idea and veered off the path towards the playground as well, I felt a sudden prickle of unease. Millie and Julia did not seem to take much notice. The pair were deep in conversation over the upcoming Carindale's Got Talent competition and were not bothered by the strange person in our midst.

All the while though, I kept an eye on him as he stood by the nearby water fountain looking our way.

Then out of the blue, Julia's surprised gasp caused both Millie and I to turn in the opposite direction.

"Is that Ryan Hodges?" Julia asked, the distress immediately obvious in her voice. "What's he doing here?"

Glancing quickly back towards the cyclist, I could see that he had already headed off on his bike and was continuing down the track. No one else at all happened to be in the area. The playground was completely deserted. There were no mothers pushing their children on swings, no one was using the basketball court and no skateboarders could be seen in the skate bowl. The place was empty. Not another person could be seen anywhere.

Except for Ryan. He seemed to have suddenly appeared but where he had come from and how he happened to be there right then, was a mystery. Perhaps he had also been on the path behind us and we hadn't realized. That seemed to be the only explanation.

The problem was though, that we had no one to call for help. Julia was clearly not comfortable around him and for that matter, neither was I. My skin was prickling once more but it was the tingling feeling at the base of my neck that I took the most notice of; that and the look of contempt on Ryan Hodge's face as he stared in our direction was what bothered me the most.

"Do you think he followed us?" Millie asked quietly.

One glance at her, told me that she was not happy with the situation either.

"He's so creepy!" she murmured fearfully. "I think we should keep going."

Julia and I instantly agreed. But we were forced to continue along the track in the direction that we'd been heading, as Ryan was blocking the path that led back home.

With Ryan's thoughts racing through my head, I hopped on my bike and hurried after my friends.

However, my energy levels were quite low and I struggled to keep up. It was the realization that Ryan was getting a kick out of scaring us, that encouraged me to pedal harder. My friends did not know what his issue was. But I did!

His evil thoughts milled around inside my own and made me more anxious than ever. He had an intense dislike for Julia and it was his aim to take advantage of her unexpected appearance back in town. He was looking for revenge and was getting a weird satisfaction out of continuing to stalk her. It also seemed that he was clearly enjoying the idea of scaring all three of us and I didn't dare turn around, even though I knew that he was close behind.

So I repeated the following words one after the other...

Keep pedaling, Emmie. That's all you can do. The girls are just up ahead. We'll be fine if we stick together. Just keep pedaling.

Saved...

Pushing on as hard as I could, it took all my strength to keep up. But when Millie and Julia disappeared around an unexpected bend in the path, I became more agitated than ever. They were so far ahead of me, and I was struggling to continue. At the same time though, the sound of the wheels on the bike behind mine was too close for comfort.

When I eventually rounded the bend, my fear worsened because the girls were nowhere in sight. It was at that point the track seemed to twist and turn as it meandered through thick bushland. Apart from the sound of my breathing and the crunch of two sets of tires on the gravel path, not another sound could be heard.

The perspiration was dripping from my forehead and once again I cursed the fact that I hadn't brought a drink bottle. Not that I would be happy to stop for a drink right then, but knowing that I had no water made me thirstier than ever.

Where are they?

The words raced through my thoughts as I kept going, pedaling as hard as I could. I knew they couldn't be too far in front, but my energy levels seemed to be dropping with each passing second.

Daring to take a quick glance back, I caught sight of Ryan a short distance behind, his bright blue bike helmet glinting in the afternoon sun. The knot in my stomach grew as I tried to maintain my steady pace but the realization that he was so close was making me ill.

That was until a familiar face flashed into view in my mind and immediately gave me the courage I needed to keep going. The image of my dad and his beaming smile had appeared out of nowhere right when I needed him most. And that's what spurred me on. Without his encouragement, I was convinced that I would not have been able to go any further.

You can do it, Emmie!

As though he were right by my side, his voice sounded clearly in my head.

Keep going, Emmie! Keep going!

Rounding the corner, I caught sight of a fork in the path. At that point, the track divided in two and led in different directions. Whether it linked up further along, I had no idea and I also had no way of knowing which path Millie and Julia had taken.

Glancing quickly back, I could see that Ryan was out of sight but would probably be rounding the bend at any moment. So I made a split second decision and veered left. Pedaling harder than ever, I continued around yet another bend and almost crashed right into Millie and Julia who had stopped dead center in the middle of the track to wait for me. And beside them was the cyclist I was concerned about earlier.

"Emmie!" Millie exclaimed. "We were just about to go and look for you. We thought you must've taken the other track."

Panting heavily, I hopped off my bike, trying to catch my breath.

"This is Tom," Julia explained as she introduced me to the cyclist standing alongside her. "He's a friend of my brother's. Such a small world to bump into him like this."

"You look so different in all your bike gear," she smiled as she indicated the professional looking gear that he was wearing. "I didn't recognize you earlier. I'm glad you're here though and we don't have to ride back on our own."

Glancing down the track, we all expected to see Ryan Hodges come hurtling around the bend. But there was no sign of anyone. And after waiting a short while longer, we guessed that he must have taken the other path.

Still trying to calm the thumping anxiety in my heart, I was at least relieved to know that we would not have to ride back alone.

And after a much-needed drink from the spare water bottle that Tom had strapped to his bike frame, I turned back in the direction that we'd come from.

However, that was when I noticed a sudden uncomfortable prickle at the base of my neck, and looking anxiously around, I felt the sensation deepen further. Convinced that Ryan was still somewhere in the area, watching and waiting, I kept my thoughts to myself and began to pedal.

I just wanted to get back home as quickly as possible.

I had no idea if he was still around but my unease stayed with me the whole way. Every now and then I took a glance back, but each time I saw no one except Matt riding along on the track behind me. Hoping desperately that we would not see Ryan again, I continued on my way. Although intuition warned me, that we should definitely be on the lookout.

I felt certain that he would appear when we least expected it.

Decisions....

The question on my mind later that night was why had Ryan been so intent on stalking Julia in the first place? And the worst thing was that he was still so obsessed with her.

It was creepy!

It reminded me of my own stalker. The way in which that man had approached my mom was the strangest part and also the most worrying. I'd been trying to forget about him in the hope that he'd just disappear and we'd never see or hear from again. But Mom wouldn't let it go. She was convinced that he had some sort of scheme in mind, although I had no idea what that could be.

The one thing I was certain of was that he had to be a mind reader too. How else would he know that the woman he'd bumped into in the grocery store was my mother? That realization was what scared me the most, especially after reading my dad's letter.

Picking up the hand-written note that I kept on my desk, I skimmed through the final paragraphs for the millionth time.

But still, no answers jumped out at me. At least I knew that my father was with me, even if only in spirit. He had been there that afternoon on the bike track and I was sure he was right there, right then, helping me in any way that he could.

Glancing at my phone, I was reminded of the other issue that had been bothering me ever since returning home that afternoon. And with the image of Jack's irresistible cheeky grin in my mind, I swiped the screen so that I could re-read his text. Again.

Hey, Emmie! I had fun hanging out with you today. Hope you enjoyed your bike ride with the girls. Let's hang out another time soon ☺

Part of me was thrilled that he'd taken the time to send it. But the other part was riddled with guilt.

After the eventful bike ride with Millie and Julia, I never did get the chance to even mention Jack's visit. By the time I returned home, I was exhausted and just wanted to collapse on the sofa. I said a quick goodbye to the girls and they continued on their way to Millie's house.

But that had made the situation even more awkward. Especially as I was sure Millie would wonder why I hadn't mentioned it.

Spending several hours, two days in a row with the boy she had a serious crush on, was not a normal thing to be doing. And I had not said a word at all to let her know.

Deciding that I needed to set things straight as soon as possible, I typed my reply.

Hey, Jack, thanks for dropping over your mom's USB. I'm really busy for the rest of the week. But maybe we can all hang out together sometime soon.

After a moment's hesitation, I pressed Send.

And then immediately wished that I hadn't.

I did not want to sound rude or mean. He certainly didn't deserve that. And I was worried he wouldn't like me anymore. But I could think of no other option.

Millie was my best friend. I had never had a best friend before and I needed to treasure that friendship, not destroy it over some silly boy crush.

Trying to convince myself that Jack and I could just be friends, I turned off my light and climbed into bed, reaching for my worn out teddy bear, the one I always turned to for comfort. Clutching it tightly to my chest, the way I had done when I was a little girl, gave me the secure feeling I was craving for.

With my eyes tightly closed, I forced away all thoughts of stalkers, mysterious men, and in particular, crushes on cute boys with drop dead gorgeous cheeky grins.

I had to believe that everything would sort itself out. It just had to. And with that thought foremost in my mind, I drifted off into a deep sleep.

The surprise text…

I didn't hear from Jack again that week. So I guessed that he had understood my message loud and clear. That hadn't helped me to feel any better about sending it though. And I wondered if he'd even speak to me when we next saw each other.

Deciding that I needed to talk to Millie and explain what had been going on, I texted her the following morning, but she and Julia were busy with rehearsals for the next few days. So I was forced to wait until the weekend to see them again.

As it turned out, explaining to Millie was even harder than I'd anticipated. Although on the outside she appeared to be okay, it was the thoughts in her head that expressed how she really felt. It was then that I knew for sure my decision to stay away from Jack, as hard as it was, had been the right one to make.

She was full of curiosity when I told her he had turned up along with his mom. I then explained how it had come about…trying to keep my voice steady and calm as if it were no big deal whatsoever.

Jack's mom needed help with her website and my mother was the perfect person for the job. It also helped to boost my mom's business so it was a win/win situation for both of them. Millie understood all of that but it was the realization that Jack had spent a couple of days hanging out at my house that surprised her the most.

She didn't say too much out loud. But her odd look in my direction summed up what she was thinking. I really didn't need to be a mind reader to work out what that was, but I decided to read her mind anyway.

At least that way, I could be one hundred percent sure.

I knew he liked Emmie. So not fair! I liked him first.

I wonder if she likes him too. But then, what sort of friend does that?

Feeling slightly uncomfortable, I changed the subject and made sure I didn't mention his name again. It was an awkward moment. The first of its kind that I'd ever experienced with Millie. I think Julia picked up on it as well and I was grateful when she changed the subject.

Turning the focus towards the competition and the new songs they'd decided on, distracted Millie, and before long the issue was forgotten. Or at least, nothing more was said. Clearly, though, I had made the right choice with the text I had sent Jack.

It also made me realize that I needed to keep my own feelings about him under control. The words 'Friend Zone' popped into my head. I was convinced once and for all, that was the way it needed to be.

But all thoughts of Jack disappeared in the next instant when we heard Millie's shocked reaction to an unexpected text on her phone. It was quite clear to both Julia and myself that she was not at all impressed to read the message that had appeared on her screen.

"OMG!" she exclaimed loudly. "Guess who is back in town?"

She stared at Julia, waiting for her response, but Julia had no idea.

"Who?" she asked, rushing quickly to Millie's side to read the message.

The shocked look on Julia's face confirmed the fact that she was just as surprised as Millie.

"What!" she exclaimed loudly. "Sara's back and wants to hang out with us? That's unbelievable. How did she even know I was here?"

I looked at the two girls in turn.

"Who's Sara?" I asked curiously.

It was Millie's response that surprised me most.

"You really don't want to know!"

Suspicions...

When Sara arrived at Millie's front door later that afternoon, I immediately realized that she was even prettier than Millie and Julia had previously indicated.

Her long blonde hair hung loosely over her shoulders and the pretty pink top she was wearing highlighted her tanned skin. The wide beaming smile that lit her face when she was introduced to me, gave me the impression that as well as being very pretty, she was also extremely friendly.

But the girls had both warned me already.

"Don't be fooled," Millie had explained earlier. "She will be really nice to your face but you have no idea what she's capable of."

Julia didn't say too much but it was clear that she agreed.

"She has made Julia's life miserable for so long. She really isn't a very nice person." Millie continued.

I soon found that Millie had lots to say on the subject of Sara. "For a while, she pretended that she'd changed and she even started being nice. But it was all fake. She'll never change. I'm just wondering why she's back so soon from her holiday in Florida. Maybe her grandparents needed a break!"

Millie laughed mockingly at that idea. Meanwhile, I wondered why Sara was keen to visit. Surely she must know how the girls felt about her.

But when she arrived at the door, I could see that was not the case. She honestly believed that they'd be happy to have her there. She seemed excited to see Julia back in town and was expecting the same reaction when the girls saw her.

I decided right then that I had never before met anyone like Sara Hamilton. Although I soon found out that in reality, she was not what she appeared on the surface. There were other things going on in her head and Millie had been right to be suspicious about her visit.

Faking...

The moment Sara and I were introduced, Sara appeared to have an avid interest in who I was.

"A new girl in town?' she asked as she looked me over.

Relieved that I'd decided to wear one of my new outfits that day, I took in the gorgeous clothes that she was wearing. Her stunning pink top had caught my eye from the beginning and it was definitely a color that suited her perfectly. The soft material was studded with a pretty sequined pattern on the front and the knit fabric held the top snugly against her body. It was such a cool style but what I admired most was her white skirt. It was fitted and fairly short with silver buttons down the front and some black stitching around the edges of the pockets.

The color and style of her outfit really showed off her tan and it was obvious that she'd been spending quite a lot of time sunbathing whilst in Florida. The thought of palm trees, crystal clear blue water and white sandy beaches came instantly to mind when she later described her visit there.

I still wondered why she had returned so soon, especially as it was her original intention to spend the entire summer with her grandparents. I was sure that if I had that opportunity, I would certainly not be rushing back. Although she explained that she'd become bored with only her grandparents for company, I was sure she was not telling us the whole truth behind her sudden arrival.

Moving on quickly from that topic, she seemed more intent on hearing all about me and where I'd come from.

As well, she was curious to find out how I'd met Millie and Julia and all about our new friendship, which she could see had come about in quite a short space of time.

When I answered all her questions, she appeared satisfied that she'd heard all she needed to know and then directed her attention towards the two girls who sat on the couch opposite, not saying a word.

"It's so good to see you both, especially you, Julia. I can't believe you're back here. Already!"

For some reason, even though I had only just met her, I was given the impression that her comment was not particularly genuine, especially the way she said the word… 'Already!' As if to ask, why are you back so soon?

But then more questions poured forth in what seemed a never-ending flow…

"What's it like out there on a farm?"

"Are there any shopping centers nearby?"

"Have you made any friends yet?"

"How on earth do you cope?"

And then came the questions that I could see she was most interested in hearing the answers to…

"How long are you staying for?"

"Have you had a chance to see Blake yet?"

"Are you guys still together?"

"Why did you come back so soon?"

When she discovered the real reason for Julia's visit, she became more interested than ever.

"Carindale's Got Talent? That sounds like fun! This is the first I've heard of it. Lucky I came over today or I might never have known it was happening. And you're entering your band?"

I could see her mind ticking over as she considered this news further. "Is there a solo division?"

When Millie responded that yes, in fact, there was a solo section for kids aged thirteen and under that both she and Jack were entering, Sara's interest grew. Then came her next question, which I had read in her mind the second before she asked it.

"It sounds like I came back just at the right time, Millie. You won't mind if I enter too, will you?"

Her sweet tone did not fool me and I caught sight of the tiny frown that had appeared on Millie's face.

Although she tried not to show it, I knew that Millie was not impressed. However, there seemed nothing she could do and that was what bothered her the most.

Secretly, I had no idea what she was worried about because Sara would have to be very good to beat Millie in a singing competition. As far as I was concerned, that would be a very difficult thing to do. And when I mentioned that to Millie, after Sara had left, she did not agree.

"Sara has a great voice," she moaned. "I can't believe she came back early. It's so typical of her to do something like this!"

When Julia and I both tried to reassure Millie and remind her of how amazing her own voice was, she explained why she was so concerned.

"I don't care if I don't win!" she exclaimed. "I just don't want Sara Hamilton to win!"

With a frustrated sigh, she shook her head and I could see the determination on her face. Beating Sara had quickly become more important than the competition itself. As far as Millie was concerned, that was all that mattered.

"I knew she was up to something," Millie complained. "I just wish I hadn't agreed that she could come over today. Why did I do that?"

Sighing helplessly, I was unable to offer any suggestions. From what I had seen that afternoon, Sara was not a genuine person. She appeared to be very friendly and likable but as Millie had said, that was all fake. She might have said nice things aloud, but her thoughts were completely different.

I had been unable to resist the temptation to read her mind. Although I've been promising myself that I'll stop, I was worried for Millie and Julia and wanted to find out the truth.

She reminded me of other girls who I'd met in the past.

The same pretty exterior, the same friendly comments, but in reality, they hadn't meant a word of what they had just said. Inside, they were nasty and mean and could definitely not be trusted.

I could clearly picture two of the girls who had fooled before. That was until I found out what they were really like.

At least I didn't need to share what I'd found out about Sara because Millie and Julia already knew. They had learned exactly what she was like and when they told me about how evil and nasty she could actually be, my sympathy grew.

I just hoped she didn't spoil Julia's visit back to her hometown.

After all, as well as entering the competition, Julia just wanted to hang out with her friends and have fun. She did not need the likes of Sara Hamilton and Ryan Hodges to ruin everything for her.

As far as Sara was concerned, she also had something else in mind. And it was that which worried me more than anything. Sara's interest in Blake had been quite obvious, to me anyway. Then when I checked her thoughts and found she'd been hoping Julia and Blake were no longer girlfriend and boyfriend, I knew for sure that she was up to no good.

The familiar uncomfortable sensation at the base of my neck had started to prickle. While I knew I had to keep my thoughts to myself, I hoped that at least there might be some way I could help. After all, I did have a huge advantage over others. I had what both my parents called a gift and perhaps it was time for me to take advantage.

My mom always said that I should use it to help others. And my dad had said the same thing. Right then, I had the feeling that the time to make good use of it may have arrived, and that I'd possibly become grateful for my gift after all.

But although I could read minds, I did not have the power to foresee the future. If I did, I would have been aware of what was ahead. And I would have been much better prepared for how to protect my friends.

Right then though, I focused on the skill that I'd been hiding away for so long and the gut instinct that seemed to appear just when I needed it.

Surely, as long as I paid attention to what was going on around me, it would be enough.

All I could do was hope that would be the case.

Shopping...

Our visit to the mall the following day was filled with surprises. Certainly ones that none of us had expected.

Millie had decided to go shopping for a new outfit for Carindale's Got Talent and when she and Julia asked me to come along, I had eagerly agreed. All three of us were determined to find the perfect choice for Millie's solo act and we decided that with each of us helping, we'd be sure to find something special.

The girls already had their outfits organized for the band's performance. It was a detail they hadn't stopped talking about and was just as important as their song choice. They'd even planned what the boys should wear as well.

But for Millie's solo, we all agreed that she needed to make a standout appearance on stage, and added to her incredible voice, this would be sure to result in a first-place prize.

Of course, ever since Sara had appeared, it had become Millie's number one goal to beat her.

At first, I thought she was taking things way too seriously and that this would prevent her from having fun. I knew that she wanted to win, but surely it was more important to enjoy the experience. However, the more Millie and Julia talked about how mean Sara had been in the past, the more I was able to understand why Millie's need to beat her was so important.

"It's not because Sara wants to enter the competition that's causing the problem," Julia explained to me while Millie was in the change room, trying on yet another pair of jeans and top that she'd found.

"It's just that we know her so well," she continued in a serious tone. "The only reason she wants to enter is because we're involved. Usually, it's me who she targets but I guess if she can't get to me, then she will just try to upset Millie. It's the next best thing. I really don't know why she has to be that way. Life is so easy for her. Everything she asks for, she gets. I just don't understand."

"I think she's jealous of you, Julia!" I replied firmly, as I looked at the bewildered girl in front of me. "I think for some reason she wants what you have. Just watch out for her. You said she's done some horrible things in the past. Well, I think she's capable of much worse."

Luckily right then, the sales assistant interrupted our conversation, asking if she could help to find sizes. Feeling myself blush slightly, I turned away from Julia. I had noticed the curious look on her face and this had added to the thoughts in her head, both of which were making me very uncomfortable.

How does Emmie know that? She only just met Sara yesterday! But she seems to know her better than I do!

I had done it again. My old habit of opening my mouth and saying too much was going to get me into trouble if I wasn't careful. Changing the subject completely, I pulled out an unusual hot pink outfit with a black fitted lace-up section around the middle that had abruptly caught my eye. I hadn't noticed it before as it was hanging towards the end of the rack hidden from view. But when I scanned the rack of clothes more thoroughly, the bright pink shade stood out vividly.

"What do you think of this, Julia? It looks like it's the last one and its Millie's size."

"Oh my gosh!" Julia exclaimed excitedly. "That looks amazing. Let's show her. I think it could be the one!"

Feeling relieved that the awkward moment had passed, I rushed towards the change room and handed the outfit over the top of the door for Millie to see. Smiling delightedly at the sound of her excited reaction, I turned back to Julia. But the curious look had returned to her face and I could hear her mind ticking over.

There's something unusual about Emmie. I'm just not sure what it is!

Ignoring her thoughtful expression, I knocked on the change room door and ordered Millie to hurry so we could see how she looked. I also wanted to move Julia's focus onto something else as quickly as possible.

Thankfully, Millie burst open the change room door and Julia and I were both overcome by the sight in front of us. The outfit was perfect and Millie's beaming smile said it all.

"I love it!" she cried happily.

It seemed that the outfit problem was solved and that should have been the perfect end to a successful day.

But we had one more important thing to do.

And it was that one important thing that happened to lead us to a whole new incident. And as is often the case, it was an incident that we could never have anticipated.

The incident...

I was the one who first spotted the girl in the designer clothing store situated towards the end of the mall. That section was where all the really expensive up-market boutiques were located. The only reason we happened to be in the area was to pick up a dress that Millie's mother had ordered the week before. The store manager had called her that morning explaining that her order had arrived. Apparently, they had managed to locate the dress in the size that she wanted and as Millie was heading to the mall that day, Mrs. Spencer had asked her to collect it and save her a trip into town.

Interestingly enough, just as we were leaving, something familiar happened to catch my eye near the entrance to the boutique next door. It must have been the flash of long blonde hair that caught my attention. I had to admit that her hair was a very distinctive feature and certainly eye-catching. The girl's back was turned but I was quite I knew who she was.

Just as I was about to nudge Millie, I noticed the girl do something very odd. In fact, I was so sure of what I'd seen that I slowed my pace and did a double take, which was probably a big mistake. Because she caught me staring and that was something I did not want.

Unable to ignore her glaring look, I gave her a small smile and hurried on my way, pretending I hadn't realized what she'd been up to. Millie and Julia were oblivious to what was going on. They had walked on ahead and I had to run to catch them.

"Don't look now but Sara's back there!" I whispered

urgently. "She's in the store next to the one we were in.

"What?" Millie asked, incredulously.

Unable to avoid the temptation, she glanced quickly back. "You mean Mimco's Designer Boutique? OMG! There is nothing in there under $250. I wonder what she's buying."

"I don't think she's buying anything," I replied in a worried tone.

Julia looked at me strangely but Millie ignored my comment and continued.

"Do you think she's looking for something to wear to the competition? Julia, you know how expensive that store is. I bet she finds something incredible."

Julia tried to reassure her and told her to stop worrying.

Surely nothing could match the outfit that was in the bag Millie was carrying. And the best part was that it had probably cost a fifth of what Sara would be spending in that store.

As I walked alongside the girls, I forced myself not to comment. Even though I had seen Sara grab the little white top off the hanger and shove it into her bag, then look guiltily around to make sure the sales assistant hadn't been watching. But there was nothing I could say or do.

As much as I wanted to tell the girls, the consequences were too risky. When Sara realized I'd spotted her, she had frozen to the spot. I know she wasn't sure if I had seen her steal the top, but it was the thoughts in her head that worried me the most.

I wonder if she saw me. If she says anything, I'll make her life hell…and her stupid friends. They'll all cop it.

I could not risk telling Millie and Julia what I had seen. I decided that the less they knew the better. If they ever indicated to Sara that they knew what she'd been up to, who knew what she might do in return.

Deciding right then, that the risk was simply not worth it, I kept my mouth closed and didn't say another word. Not about the topic of Sara, that was. Her name wasn't mentioned again until later that afternoon at Millie's house.

It was Ryan Hodge's name that came up next.

Just in case...

"What is he doing here?" Millie asked with a frown.

She had spotted the one person we definitely wanted to avoid. Right there in the middle of the food court, staring at us as we sat eating our lunch, was the familiar dark-haired boy with the continual evil smirk plastered to his face.

"He's just trying to frighten us," I responded quietly. "Just ignore him. If he knows that he's bothering us, he'll keep it up."

Of course, I knew exactly what was going in Ryan's mind and exactly what his intentions were. I just had to convince Millie and Julia to follow my advice.

"Lucky Blake's not around," Julia's look of concern was becoming more intense as she glanced from the corner of her eye towards the kid who was causing so much trouble.

"I haven't told Blake what happened on our bike ride," she continued. "But if this keeps up, maybe I should tell him what's going on. I don't want him getting into another fight. But I don't want Ryan stalking me the whole time I'm here, either."

Biting my lip, I replied, unable to keep the worry from my voice. "Maybe it's not a good idea to tell Blake yet, Julia. How about we just try ignoring Ryan and see if that works first."

She nodded her head reluctantly in agreement but I could see that she was not totally convinced. Although I could hardly blame her. I had experienced the feeling of being stalked and I knew first-hand what that was like.

An image of the mystery mind-reading man dressed in his dirty long black coat flashed through my mind and I shuddered in response. At least there had been no sign of him lately, although every time I was anywhere near the mall, I was on edge. That fear was something I found hard to deal with. I would never admit it to my mom but I constantly found myself glancing over my shoulder just to be sure he was nowhere in sight.

Unfortunately, though, I had the sneaking suspicion he was around. Even though I couldn't see him, I could feel his presence, watching and waiting. For what, I had no idea, and that was what scared me.

I guessed Julia was feeling much the same way about Ryan. And that was not a nice feeling at all.

Quickly we finished our meal and made our way out of the mall towards the bus stop, in order to catch a bus back to Millie's house.

We were all slightly afraid and each of us kept a lookout.

Just in case.

Book 3

The Promise

Guilt...

A mountain of scorching flames soared high into the sky. Above the deafening roar could be heard the distant wail of fire engines but I knew there was no way they'd make it in time.

My heart pounded wildly and I was engulfed with fear. Waves of misery clutched at the pit of my stomach and I could feel beads of sweat dripping from my skin. Ignoring the suffocating heat and the racing of my pulse, I crouched out of sight behind a nearby clump of trees.

How could I have allowed this to happen?

How could I have stood by and done nothing?

I was as guilty as the person who had lit the match and I knew I'd regret my stupidity for the rest of my life.

But right then it was too late.

All I could do was stand helplessly by and watch.

Confrontation...

As I stood there helpless, but at the same time transfixed by the raging fire, I was taken back; back in time to the events that had led up to this fateful day. And in a torrent of waves, the memories flashed through my thoughts.

We'd been at the bus stop, waiting to catch a bus to Millie's house. So much had happened that day and when we spotted Ryan for the second time, we were convinced he was stalking us. Well, stalking Julia that was.

At least that's the way it seemed. And afterward, I wondered if we had tried to be friendly to him, perhaps the outcome may have been very different.

But instead, sick to death of his constant lurking, Julia had let loose. I didn't blame her in the slightest. Ryan deserved every bit of what she said to him. And it was about time he was told to simply back off and stay away.

"Just leave me alone!" she yelled, the disgust and anguish clear in her voice.

At first she was angry, and I could see that she'd begun to let fly with everything she had. The thoughts swirling in her head were full of hatred for this annoying boy. She had done nothing to deserve his torment and just wanted him to go away. But then her thoughts had become fearful and her tone abruptly changed.

"Can't you see I don't want anything to do with you? Please, just go away and leave me alone. That's all I ask!"

Rather than a demand, it had become a plea for mercy and when I looked at Ryan, it was easy to see why. His expression had turned to one of fury and my eyes darted protectively back towards Julia.

We were all waiting for him to respond, although my immediate impulse was to run away and escape the look of pure hatred that seemed to pour out of him. The atmosphere around us had suddenly became so tense...each of us stood frozen to the spot.

He did not say a word, not out loud anyway. But I knew exactly what he was thinking.
And the words that filled his head made my blood turn cold.

"You're going to pay for what you've done. You won't think you're so cool...you and your friends are gonna be sorry!"

Even though the words were whispered in his thoughts, I still felt the power and the evil that emanated from them. Each syllable was filled with hatred; hatred for Julia and for Blake, whose name he whispered with sheer contempt. Then he went on to include both Millie and me in his silent threat, just for being Julia's friends and a part of her world.

How it was possible for a person to feel such intensely horrible emotions towards others was beyond me. Even though I had been bullied terribly in the past, I had never felt the emotions that Ryan was filled with.

For a brief moment, I felt sorry for him. But my fear of what he was capable of, overcame any sympathy and that feeling quickly disappeared.

What concerned me most was how to protect my friends. As my mom had told me on several occasions, I had a gift and must learn how to use it. Well, it seemed the time had come. The problem was...I was completely at a loss for what to do.

The revelation...

Later that afternoon at Millie's house, we told her mom what had happened. The Ryan situation had obviously gone too far and something needed to be done. Millie's mother, who seemed to know pretty much everything that went on in Carindale, told us that Ryan and his mom had moved to the other side of town and she was surprised that we had bumped into him.

It appeared to me that as soon as Ryan realized Julia was back, he was making it his life mission to stalk her and cause her as much misery as possible. It was a form of payback for the problems he'd faced at school, and he wanted revenge. Julia's return to Carindale had given him a golden opportunity.

Mrs. Spencer, however, had the impression that we were over-reacting. I knew exactly what was going on in her head and her thoughts did not match the words coming out of her mouth.

She'd promised to talk to Mr. Spencer and perhaps take a visit to Ryan's house to speak with his mom about what was going on. But I knew she wasn't taking the situation as seriously as she should. And unfortunately, I was unable to tell her everything I'd heard him say, the words that I was sure would make her finally sit up and take notice.

After a few words of reassurance, telling us that we should just stay together and avoid Ryan if we saw him, she then continued on with some news of her own. And within no time, all thoughts of Ryan had been cast aside.

This new piece of information was so surprising, that each of us became speechless with disbelief.

Millie and Julia sat open-mouthed, staring at Mrs. Spencer for a few moments until their brains registered fully what she had told us. Even though I didn't know Sara the way they did, I was just as surprised as my friends to hear what she had been up to.

It turned out that Mrs. Spencer had bumped into Sara's mom at the grocery store earlier that morning. And when Mrs. Spencer asked how Sara was, Sara's mom burst into tears.

"It was such a shock," Mrs. Spencer said, as she looked at each of us in turn. "I certainly hadn't expected that reaction. I was so surprised when she began to cry, right there in the grocery store in full view of everyone. And as soon as I asked if she was okay, she just came right out with all the details about Sara. Apparently, she and her husband have been having so many problems with her, and it seemed that she just wanted someone to talk to. She said that because Sara's been such a handful at home they decided to send her on vacation to stay with her grandparents in Florida, hoping that a break would be good for her. But Sara only lasted a couple of weeks because she was caught shoplifting, of all things!"

"Shoplifting?" Millie gasped, immediately looking to Julia whose eyes were wide with surprise.

I stared at the girls, just as surprised as they were to hear this startling news. And instantly I thought back to the shoplifting incident I'd witnessed myself just that day. Although I had a sudden impulse to tell them exactly what I'd seen, I quickly clamped my mouth closed, deciding that it was not a good idea.

When Mrs. Spencer noticed our shocked reactions, she swore each of us to secrecy. "Girls, the only reason I'm telling you is that I think Sara probably needs her friends right now. Her parents are at their wit's end and have no idea what to do. Sara is obviously going through a difficult time, but maybe you girls can try to help her."

When Millie opened her mouth to protest, Mrs. Spencer immediately cut her short. "I know you've had altercations with Sara in the past, Millie, but surely you can put that behind you. Just try to be a friend to her and I'm certain you'll see a different side to the poor girl."

Millie opened her mouth once more. I could clearly see that she was not at all impressed with her mother's suggestion. But she obviously knew she would be wasting her time arguing, and rather than complain, she just rolled her eyes and shook her head.

"Whatever!" The word was whispered under her breath so that her mom didn't hear it. And when Millie glanced our way, she firmly shook her head, the disgust clear on her face.

I could see straight away that there was no way Mrs. Spencer could persuade Millie to change her mind. Both she and Julia had tried on several occasions to become friendly with Sara but each time it had backfired disastrously. It was quite obvious that Sara would never have their support again.

Julia and I followed Millie to her room, where she closed the door so we could talk in private.

"Can you believe that?" Millie asked, her mouth agape once more. "Sara Hamilton caught shoplifting! It's almost a joke!"

"I know," Julia replied. "The whole thing is so crazy! And can you believe that her mother told your mom! If Sara knew, she'd be furious!"

I watched the two girls as the comments flew back and forth between them. They were in absolute shock and for that matter, so was I! According to Mrs. Spencer, Sara had been caught for stealing a designer jacket from a really expensive store in an exclusive part of town. But because her grandmother is a regular customer of that store, the manager decided to let Sara off with just a warning. Her grandparents were so humiliated and embarrassed that they insisted Sara return home. And they booked her a ticket on the next available flight.

Mrs. Spencer said that Sara's mom was really upset. She had no idea what was going on or why her daughter would even contemplate such a thing. The strangest part was that there was no need for her to steal in the first place. Her grandmother would probably have bought her the jacket if she'd asked. Then the whole issue could have been avoided.

Thinking back to what I'd witnessed myself earlier that day, I blurted out impulsively. "I saw her steal a top at the shopping center today as well."

"What?" Millie and Julia gasped once more.

"You're kidding? What top? Where from?" Millie's words tumbled out, followed by Julia's startled response.

"From Mimco's Boutique? You actually saw her take something? And she got away with it?" Julia was shaking her head with concern. This situation was quickly becoming much worse.

"Unbelievable," she continued. "Her mom gives her so much money, she could buy anything she wanted. Why is she stealing? It just doesn't make sense!"

"Wait! Does she know that you saw her?" Millie exclaimed suddenly. "Maybe we should tell someone before she causes trouble!"

"NO!" I exclaimed quickly.

Both girls stared at me, a look of confusion on each of their faces.

"I mean…I'm not sure if we should say anything. Who would we tell, anyway? If her mom finds out, she'll just be more upset and I'm sure it won't help anything." I looked from Millie to Julia and back again, the sick feeling in my stomach abruptly becoming much worse.

I'd opened my big mouth and told them what I had seen when I should have kept it to myself. Taking a deep breath, I continued.
"I'm not sure it's a good idea to say anything. And I don't think we should let Sara know either. We all know what she's capable of."

I looked at both my friends, hoping they would agree. As I watched the hesitation in Julia's expression, I could see that she was thinking about what I'd said.

"Well with the competition coming up and all, I guess we don't want to stir up any trouble. Maybe we should just stay quiet for now."

Julia glanced at Millie, waiting for her approval. But I could see that Millie was not so sure.

"Alright!" she eventually sighed. "We'll keep it secret for now. And let's just stay as far away from her as possible. That girl is trouble!"

Breathing a quick sigh of relief, I nodded my head in agreement.

Staying away from Sara was definitely a good idea.
But none of us realized right then how hard that was going to be!

The surprise...

Before leaving Millie's later that afternoon, Julia received a call from Blake announcing a party that he and Jack had been invited to on the following Saturday night. And Julia and Millie were invited as well.

Hayden, one of their friends from school, was celebrating his thirteenth birthday. Because he was officially becoming a teenager, his parents had given him permission to have a big party and invite a heap of friends. And to make it extra special, his mom had suggested they have a theme, so it had been decided that everyone should go in fancy dress costume.

At Julia's insistence, Blake contacted Hayden to find out if I could go along as well. Both Julia and Millie were really hoping that he'd say yes, and this, of course, was what I was hoping for as well. The thought of a costume party was so exciting, especially as I had never been to one before.

While we waited for an answer, I sat with the girls, each of them trying to figure out what they'd wear. They only had a few days to get organized which didn't allow much time to find an outfit. But then Julia jumped up from her spot on Millie's bed and pulled open the cupboard doors. Scanning the interior, she looked for something that would work.

"Millie has so many clothes. There's sure to be something in here that we can put together to dress up in."

Glancing over her shoulder, I gaped at the variety of clothes hanging in the cupboard.

Julia certainly hadn't exaggerated and I took in the array of colors as well as the numerous piles of tops, jackets, jeans, t-shirts, belts and other accessories, neatly stacked on the adjoining shelves.

There seemed to me to be too much to choose from, but within seconds Julia had pulled out a variety of clothes, making suggestions about each of them.

Taking a dress from its hanger, she held it up. "This dress could work as a pirate outfit," she laughed. "It's a perfect style and I'm sure with an eye patch and a scarf, it'd look great."

Throwing the dress on the bed, she continued her search, "What about this red top with your black leggings, Millie? You could go as a super hero. All you'd need is a cape and a mask. That would look amazing on you!"

Julia's eyes lit up as the ideas raced around in her head and I admired her ability to be able to think of so many choices with such little effort. The suggestions poured from her one after the other, which was something I knew I would definitely not be capable of. I really had no idea how she did it.

In no time, there were a variety of outfits laid out on the bed in front of us, and both girls stood back deciding which one to wear.

Just then, Julia's phone rang again and Millie and I waited silently for her to finish her call.

"It's all good!" she said grinning excitedly at me, as she disconnected the call and put down her phone. "Hayden said its fine for you to go. He doesn't mind at all."

Beaming happily, I looked from Julia to Millie.
This was the best news I'd heard all day, and I was so
grateful to be invited.

My level of excitement increased even more when Millie
picked up the "pirate" dress and handed it to me. "You
should wear this! It would look incredible on you, Emmie!"

Smiling even wider, I looked at the dress that I had already
been admiring. It was the one outfit I'd had my eye on and I
could not believe my luck.

"Are you sure, Millie? You won't mind if I borrow it?"

"Of course not," she replied quickly. "Don't be silly. Why
don't you try it on and see how it looks?"

With a grateful grin, I did as she suggested and soon found
that it fitted me perfectly. Although the length was cut
shorter than I would have liked, I decided that I could wear
a little pair of shorts underneath. I also knew it would be
very easy to make a pirate eye patch out of cardboard, to set
it off. Then I would definitely look like a pirate.
Excitement filled the room. Millie and Julia chose outfits for
themselves and we chatted about how much fun it was
going to be to dress up in costume.

There was also something else that I was thrilled about. It
had just occurred to me, and I could hardly wait for
Saturday night to arrive.

I hadn't seen Jack at all since the day he'd been at my house
and although I knew I should keep my distance, it hadn't
stopped me from thinking about him. If I were to be
completely honest, I'd have to admit that not one day had
gone by when I hadn't pictured his handsome face and

cheeky smile.

Earlier this week, my mom asked me what I was smiling about. "What is that grin for Emmie? You look deep in thought, but whatever it is, it certainly looks like something good!"

I turned bright red in response and pretended I was thinking of something else. Even though I sometimes shared my innermost secrets with my mom, I was not at all comfortable talking about my crush on Jack. *Probably because I felt so guilty about it.*

But I missed not hanging out with him and ever since his last text, I had not seen or heard from him at all. And that was something that had been worrying me. We'd had so much fun together but when he wanted to hang out some more, I made up an excuse and said I was too busy.

The reason, of course, was that I knew Millie liked him. So it was the wrong thing for me to be hanging out with him, even if we were just friends. I was sure that she wouldn't be happy about the situation and I did not want a boy to come between us. I still thought I'd made the right choice about avoiding him, but it hadn't helped me to feel any better about it.

As I waved goodbye to Millie and Julia, pangs of guilt settled in my stomach. There I was with the dress that Millie had loaned me tucked away in a plastic bag under my arm, and all I could think about was seeing Jack again. I really needed to quit obsessing over the boy she liked.

With a sigh, I forced all thoughts of Jack to the rear of my mind, keeping them tucked secretly away for another time. I was definitely looking forward to seeing Jack again, but

Millie's friendship was what mattered most, and that was something I needed to remember.

The sighting...

Chatting excitedly to my mom as I sat in the front seat of our car alongside her, I told her all about the upcoming party and then described the events of the day. There was a heap to tell her because so much had happened in such a short space of time. It had definitely been a day full of surprises but I soon found out that the surprises were yet to end.

As we turned into our street and headed in the direction of our house, I caught sight of one person I had temporarily forgotten about. But as soon as I spotted that familiar black coat, I knew instantly who he was.

Glancing nervously out the window as we drove by, I felt a sinking anxiety working its way into the pit of my stomach. He was standing stock still, staring directly at me. Turning my head quickly away, I could feel his eyes follow our car. I knew beyond a doubt he'd been watching and waiting. Waiting for me to show up.

But where had he come from and how did he know where we lived? And most importantly, what was he doing there?

When I got out of the car, however and looked back down the street, there was no sign of him anywhere.

Had I just imagined it? Had he really been there and then simply disappeared without a trace? Could that even be possible?

Gripping tightly to the plastic bag with the pirate dress safely intact, I made my way up the driveway towards our front door...a prickling sensation niggling the skin at the base of my neck.

I knew that I should tell my mom about what I'd seen. But the problem was, it was likely I'd imagined it. And the more I thought about it, the more I convinced myself that my imagination had probably been running wild.

That was the only explanation for what I thought was his sudden appearance and the way in which he had abruptly disappeared.

There was also no reason for him to be standing on our street in the first place.

Or was there?

Although I tried to brush the worry from my mind, it remained lurking there the entire night and I was unable to overcome the fear that had taken hold.

Before going to bed, I checked and double-checked that my window was securely locked and then raced back down the stairs to be sure that the house was secure.

Moving from window to window and then from the front door to the back door, I made my way methodically through the house, also taking time for a quick peek out onto the street. It looked deserted.

At first, my mom was just curious. "Emmie, what are you doing? You know I always make sure the house is locked up before I go to bed!"

When I ignored her and continued on my mission, she questioned me further. "Emmie, did you hear what I said?"

It was then that I decided to make up a story. I did not want her worrying about the strange man. If he had really been standing on our street corner and I hadn't imagined it, there was not too much we could do right then. So I decided there was no point in mentioning him to her.

Instead, I pretended that I'd heard about some break-ins just down the road over the last few days and that I was taking precautions. I wasn't too sure she believed my story because she frowned and told me that she hadn't heard anything.

Regardless of whether or not she was satisfied with my explanation, I ignored her concerned expression and hugged her goodnight. Wanting to avoid any further questions or comments, I headed back to my room and closed the door firmly behind me.

The sound of the wind whistling through the night and scraping tree branches against my window added to my unease. Eventually, though, I was able to clear my mind of images of creepy men with dark, intense eyes and long black coats, and drift into a restless sleep.

The party...

Finally, the evening of the party arrived and after some doubts about my outfit, I was persuaded by my mom that with the help of the eye mask and a pirate style gun that Millie had found in a dress-up box, I really did look like a pirate.

When I heard the honk of Millie's car horn in the driveway, I raced excitedly out the front door.

Sitting in the back seat of the car, we admired each other's costumes. Millie had decided to go as a super hero after all and Julia was dressed as a witch. Millie had worn the witch costume at a school Halloween disco last year.

I remembered seeing the Halloween photo of the two girls, on the shelf in Millie's bedroom. It had looked great on Millie and it looked amazing on Julia as well.

Dressing up in costume certainly made everything so much more fun, and we were all wondering what the boys would be dressed as. They'd kept their choices a secret, with Blake telling Julia they wanted to surprise us all. As the car headed along the suburban streets, I thought once again of Jack's cheeky smile and I was certain that whatever costume he wore, he'd look great in it.

When I told the girls that it was the first party I'd been to in a very long time, they looked at me with surprise. Then when I admitted that I'd only ever been invited to one birthday party before, and that was back when I was eight years old, they sat staring silently, not sure what to say.

The thoughts in their heads were ones of pity. I was a girl who had lived such a different life to each of them and I knew they found it hard to comprehend. They didn't want to admit that parties were a regular occurrence in Carindale and that each of them celebrated their own birthdays with a party of some description almost every year. I read their thoughts and imagined in my own mind, all the fun celebrations they'd enjoyed while growing up.

A memory of my own then came to mind, but it wasn't a happy one and was certainly nothing like the ones floating through the minds of the girls alongside me. The one birthday party that I was invited to so many years earlier had ended in disaster. It was the eighth birthday of a girl in my class whose name was Megan. At that stage, I hadn't learned to keep quiet about all the thoughts going on in the heads of the people around me; and that was what had caused all the drama.

Without thinking, I'd blurted out the location of the treasure in the treasure hunt and that particular game was over before it had even begun. Megan's mom had been standing by watching, and her thoughts had easily worked their way into my own. I remember her looking at me crossly and thinking, "Oh, great! After all the effort in setting up this game and deciding on the best hiding spot, thanks to that girl, it ended in about two seconds flat!"

She clearly was not impressed and neither was Megan, who told me outright that I'd spoiled the game.

Then to make matters worse, I told Megan that her so-called best friend was only pretending to like her. I thought I was helping and that Megan should know the truth.

I even shared the other girl's exact thoughts, out loud so that everyone could hear. *"This is such a dumb party. I wish I hadn't come!"*

The girl turned a bright shade of red and then denied it. Meanwhile, Megan had run off to her bedroom crying.

Megan's mom overheard the whole conversation but all she could do was shake her head at me and frown. It was immediately obvious that she thought I was a troublemaker and I was never invited to Megan's place again. Megan and her friends stopped playing with me at school and they made sure no one else played with me either.

"She's weird," I heard Megan telling a group of kids one day. "And she wrecked my party. Just stay away from her!"

After this disaster, I'd taken on a loner status at school. After a while, I began to accept the fact that no one wanted anything to do with me.

Although I knew I was to blame, it took me quite a while to learn from my mistakes. I was just grateful that finally, I knew to keep my mouth closed. Reminding myself of the promise I'd made to myself only a few weeks before, I mentally created an invisible brick wall in my mind. I hadn't been using it too much lately, but I definitely did not want to spoil another birthday party, nor did I want to draw attention to myself. So that was all the encouragement I needed.

When the car pulled into the curb outside Hayden's house and we all climbed from the back seat onto the pavement, I made sure the invisible wall was intact. Then I followed Millie and Julia past the brightly lit garden area towards the front door. Feeling a little self-conscious in my outfit, I walked through the open front door of the house where we were greeted by Hayden who was dressed as a Star Wars character.

I took an instant liking to the friendly boy, who welcomed us inside and directed us to the large family room at the back of the house. We soon discovered it had been decorated with balloons and streamers and had really cool flashing lights hanging from the ceiling. This created such a cool party atmosphere and we all looked around in admiration.

There were already several other kids there, none of whom I knew, and I stayed close by Millie and Julia. But they had spotted some friends from school and made their way towards them. For Julia, it was a great chance to catch up with kids who she had not had seen since school had ended. They all appeared equally excited to see both her and Millie and within seconds, the two girls were the center of attention. Blake had also arrived and a big group of kids and everyone gathered together welcoming each other. Feeling a little out of place, I stood shyly aside and glanced awkwardly around the room. And that was when I spotted Jack.

Feeling a small tremor of excitement, I glanced across at him and watched for a moment. He hadn't noticed me and I was able to look on without him knowing as he laughed and chatted with some friends.

Dressed as a rapper, he definitely looked the part. It was a perfect choice for him, especially as rap music was the style he loved. I thought that he looked more handsome than ever. His oversized t-shirt was a really cool style and he also wore a red cap facing backward on his head. From where I was standing, I had the urge to go over and tug on the cap. Maybe even pull it right off and then spin around as if it wasn't me and I'd had nothing to do with it. Grinning at the thought, I pictured his reaction and imagined his look of surprise.

I continued to watch him from my spot across the room, not realizing I was staring. That was until he abruptly turned his head and instantly our eyes met.

Feeling an embarrassed flush of red creep rapidly over my skin, I looked quickly away and tried to pretend I hadn't been staring at all. But at the same time, from the corner of my eye, I could see him making his way towards me.

The butterflies in my stomach were doing crazy somersaults and I was forced to gulp down a breath of air to try and calm my racing pulse. It was a mixture of nerves and excitement that I was struggling to control.

But when I felt a small tug on my sleeve, I looked up to see his beautiful brown eyes staring into my own.

"Hey!" he said, grinning widely, "You look awesome!"

"Thanks!" I responded shyly, not sure what else to say.

But secretly, I was pleased that he liked my costume, and I smiled with delight.

"You look great too." Still trying to control the nerves jumping around inside my stomach, I glanced up at his hat, and found the courage to say, "Your outfit is so cool!"

"I'm glad you like it!" It was obvious he was happy that I approved and his eyes locked on mine as he continued on. "I was thinking of wearing these clothes for Carindale's Got Talent. What do you think?"

"That'd be perfect!" I nodded, feeling more comfortable by the second. "You look like a total rapper in that. It's such a great choice."

He had a way of putting me at ease whenever I was near him and all anxious thoughts melted away. The fact that he was actually interested in my opinion really meant a lot and I could tell that he was genuinely pleased with my approval of his clothes. We seemed to connect so easily and I felt a sudden bubbling of happiness welling up inside me.

Millie was standing by my side chatting to some other friends but when she noticed who I was talking to, she grinned happily as well. She didn't seem the least bit concerned that I was talking to Jack and that all his attention right then was focused on me.

But it was what she whispered in my ear that surprised me the most. "Jack likes you!"

Once again, I felt my face flush red and then my mouth dropped open in response. I certainly had not been

expecting to hear those words from her and at first, I thought I had misunderstood.
The music was loud and it was hard to hear, especially because she was whispering.

"It's so obvious," she added, the smile still evident on her face.

I didn't know what to say and shook my head slightly in denial. Gulping anxiously, I opened my mouth to speak, but before I had a chance to reply, Millie squeezed my arm encouragingly, the smile remaining fixed to her face. But then, distracted by all the kids around her, she looked away and continued chatted excitedly with the group.

Although she hadn't really said so, it was quite clear she was having a great time and the thought of Jack liking me didn't seem to bother her at all. It was something I had never expected and it took a moment to process the meaning of her words. Taking a deep breath, I smiled. I smiled at Millie and her friends and I smiled at Jack; the happiness I was feeling right then seemed to overflow. It was such a wonderful sensation and I could hardly believe how good I felt in that moment.

While I wasn't completely sure that Jack really did like me, I suspected that he did and I certainly hoped that it true. But the main reason for my happiness right then was that Millie was okay with it all. To me, that was what mattered the most.

If Jack and I could hang out and have fun together, without me feeling guilty and worrying that I would upset Millie, then that was the best thing ever.

The party was shaping up to be loads of fun and a group of

girls had started dancing. It seemed that nothing at all could go wrong.

But then, at the turn of just about every head in the room, we glanced behind us, curious to see what had suddenly caught everyone's attention.

And the atmosphere amongst my group of friends changed completely.

Sara...

Dressed in an amazing costume, Sara entered the room. With almost every pair of eyes looking her way, she beamed with excitement, reveling in the attention she was receiving by her late entrance.

She looked amazing. That was something we all had to admit. But instantly I felt sorry for Julia who had also dressed as a witch. While Julia looked really pretty in her costume, Sara seemed to outshine everyone in the room. What made matters worse was that she knew it.

She was carrying a straw broom and wore some really cool, super long, over the knee socks that were striped in vivid blue and purple. This was the exact same color as the rest of her costume and even though the length of the dress was very short, it really did look incredible.

I noticed that several boys were staring at her as well, and this included Blake and Jack. I couldn't help but feel a twinge of jealousy and when I glanced towards Millie, she rolled her eyes in disgust.

"Typical for her to arrive looking like that!" Millie whispered in my ear.

"I wouldn't mind so much," she continued, "but she obviously loves herself to death. Can't you tell?"
I had to agree with Millie as I watched Sara prance across the room. She headed straight for Hayden, the birthday boy, and handed him a beautifully wrapped gift.

Despite the large crowd of kids scattered around, she managed to be the center of attention and it was clear to me that was exactly what she'd hoped for.

Choosing to ignore her, Millie and Julia turned back to their group of friends and continued chatting. But Julia was shaking her head and the look of dismay on her face showed exactly how she felt about Sara's sudden arrival. I understood completely, especially with all the issues Julia had experienced with Sara in the past, constantly wanting to outdo her.

I also had a sneaking suspicion that Sara may have been forewarned somehow, and was aware that Julia was planning to dress as a witch. I guessed there could have been any number of ways that she may have found out.

Perhaps Millie's mom had been speaking to Sara's mother again. Or maybe one of the boys may have bumped into her and let it slip. I really had no idea, but I had the distinct feeling that she'd chosen her costume intentionally and in the process, made sure that her outfit was the stand out one of the two.

I was curious about the gift Sara had given Hayden. It appeared to be a very large box and was beautifully wrapped. I couldn't help but wonder what on earth could be inside it.

Millie, Julia and I, who had decided to combine our money and give Hayden something from the three of us, had been at a loss for what to choose. But then Blake had suggested one of the latest computer games, which he assured us Hayden would love. This game, in particular, was usually quite expensive but we'd managed to get it on sale when we visited the store, so we were very lucky.

Hopefully, no one else at the party had thought of the same idea. But we were yet to find that out, as our gift was sitting on a nearby table along with other presents that he'd been given but had not yet opened.

Just as I turned back to Jack and the others, I heard Sara's distinctive voice behind me. "Hi, girls! Great to see you all!"

I glanced in the direction of the sound and acknowledged her uncomfortably. Julia and Millie looked towards her as well, but I could see they were not at all happy to have her join them.

"You all look so great!" she exclaimed excitedly, as she glanced briefly at each of us in turn. Then her gaze stopped on Julia. "And I see that we're both witches, Julia. What a coincidence!"

Julia smiled but did not respond. This, however, didn't stop Sara, and I was sure that I'd noticed a confident but satisfied smirk brush across her face. Clearly pleased at Julia's annoyed reaction, she kept talking, at the same time ensuring that she had the avid attention of our entire group. It was as though she had heaps to say and was determined to have everyone listen in and not miss a single word.

"Blake and Jack, you boys look fantastic!"

She stared admiringly at the two of them, beaming widely. But then her gaze seemed to focus directly on Blake, and I had the distinct feeling that she was more interested in him than she should be. Especially as he was Julia's boyfriend.

From the corner of my eye, I took in Julia's response, and I could see her glaring with frustration. But although Julia was clearly not impressed, Sara continued on regardless.

With a slight shake of my head, I looked at Millie and raised my eyebrows in disbelief. I was beginning to see what the girls had warned me about. Added to what I'd witnessed at the mall and also what we'd heard regarding Sara's behavior in Florida, I had decided that I wanted as little to do with Sara as possible.

She was clearly a troublemaker and I made a quick decision to take down my inner mental barrier so I could figure out exactly what was going on in her head. At least that way, I would have a good idea of what she was planning. But when her thoughts came crashing into my own, I gasped in horror.

"Are you okay?" Jack asked me with a frown. He'd heard my quick intake of breath and was concerned there was something wrong. When I felt several other pairs of eyes staring towards me as well, Sara's included, I mumbled a vague response, pretending that everything was fine.

I was given some odd glances but avoided having to explain myself because the volume of the music suddenly became much louder. Turning towards the center of the room, we could see that Hayden's parents were encouraging everyone to form a line and play the limbo game. In that moment, Sara was forgotten as the majority of kids in the room rushed to be amongst the first to line up.

I remained standing where I was, however, as I was shocked at what I'd found out. The more I learned about Sara, the more concerned about her I became and I was at a loss for what to do.

But I was given no further time to consider any kind of a solution because Jack abruptly grabbed my hand and dragged me into the line of laughing kids. Momentarily putting Sara out of my mind, I followed behind the others and headed towards the limbo stick. Then, copying their lead, I leaned over backward to pass beneath it. I had never played the game before, but it was a heap of fun and all negative thoughts disappeared.

With loud music playing in the background and everyone singing to the latest hit song, the room was full of noise and laughter. And then the limbo stick was lowered and the game became more serious. We all soon discovered that it was harder and harder to pass beneath without bumping it and soon only a few kids remained in the line.

Standing to the side alongside Millie, Jack and the others who had also been eliminated, we looked on as the last remaining kids who were still in the line continued to make their way under the stick. Still in were Julia, Blake and Sara and the game became more and more exciting as the stick was lowered further each time they all passed underneath.

It amazed me how flexible each person was and how low they could bend backward. Everyone was cheering them on and it became even more exciting as they continued. Of course, Millie and I were hoping that Julia would win. But in actual fact, we would have been happy to see anyone win; anyone, except Sara, who was enjoying every minute she spent with Blake at her side.

When they ended up being the last two remaining, however, all we could do was watch her in action.

"Come on, Blake!" Sara called in her sickly sweet and encouraging voice. "You can do it!"

But when Blake happened to touch the stick and then Sara was announced the final winner, she threw her arms around him in an excited hug.

Blake, however, obviously uncomfortable with all the attention she was giving him, did his best to shrug away from her. He then quickly made his way to Julia's side and took a firm hold of her hand.

Standing aside, I could see that Sara was annoyed to be brushed off in that manner. But she deserved it and I did a silent cheer for Blake for not showing any interest. With a roll of her eyes as if not bothered in the slightest, she turned to follow Hayden's mom so she could claim her prize as the winner.

Thankfully though, that seemed to put an end to her flirting, at least with Blake. And much to our relief, she spent the remainder of the night with a completely different group of kids. Although I did spot her looking Blake's way on several occasions.

While the rest of the party was filled with several other games, including musical chairs and musical statues, where everyone had to freeze on the spot when the music stopped, I was unable to avoid hearing the thoughts that continued working their way through Sara's head.

She was definitely fixated on Blake and I was quite sure that there would be no stopping her. How she could seriously behave that way, I really had no idea. But I realized that somehow I'd have to warn Julia.

I just needed to figure a way to do it.

Afterthoughts...

When I climbed into bed later that night, I thought back to what had unfolded at the party.

From the moment that Sara had arrived, it seemed all she wanted was to get Blake's attention. And knowing exactly what she had in mind, made it harder than ever for me to enjoy myself as I watched her in action.

More than anything, she wanted Blake for herself. To have him like her more than Julia was what mattered most. And I could not work out whether she genuinely liked him or if her main aim was to upset Julia in the meanest way possible.

The horrible thoughts floating through her mind just before we left the party continued to haunt me. And I almost wished I hadn't read her mind at all. It was just too upsetting.

"When Julia's gone, it'll be so easy. I'll have Blake all to myself and it'll serve her right! She never deserved him anyway!"

Sighing loudly, I pulled the bed covers up to my chin. The night had turned cool and I snuggled down deeper for warmth. Or perhaps it was the thought of getting to know Sara and what she was capable of, that was making me so uncomfortable.

I knew I should tell Julia what I'd found out. Whether or not she already suspected anything, I had no idea, but I thought she deserved to be warned. The problem was, once Julia left town, what could be done to stop Sara from following through on her silent threat?

I just hoped that Blake would stay loyal to Julia. It would be terrible if Sara won out in the end. To me, it just didn't seem right.

With another sigh, Jack's irresistible grin popped into my head and I switched my thoughts completely; grateful for the distraction.

That was all I needed for the smile return to my face, the same smile that had been stuck there earlier, when he and I had stood side by side, talking, laughing and just having fun.

For me, those moments had been magical.

And that was what kept me smiling until I eventually fell asleep, images of Jack's smiling face floating through my head and into my dreams.

The warning...

I woke to the sound of a text on my phone. I could feel a smile lingering on my lips and was kind of annoyed to have been disturbed. I'd been having the most incredible dream and rolled over to try and recover the images that had been so clear in my head. But already they were fading away and all I had were a few snippets to remember my dream by.

Jack was sitting alongside me and whispering something in my ear. Then without warning, he wrapped his arm around me and pulled me close. I could still feel the warmth of his presence beside me and the secure sensation of finally feeling safe. And then, he looked into my eyes and smiled.

That was when I was woken by the text on my phone and the dream had abruptly ended. But nothing would bring it back. It was over and all I could do was try to hold on to the vision that was already becoming a blur.

Giving up on any chance to go back to that blissful state, I reached for my phone and looked at the screen. When I spotted the pink love heart, I knew straight away that it was a text from Millie.

Hey, Emmie! Do you want to come to the movies with us? A big group of kids from the party are planning to meet at the cinema at 11. Blake and Jack are coming too. ☺

She ended the text with a winky face emoticon. And I chuckled quietly to myself, knowing exactly what she was referring to. Once again, I felt very grateful that she was encouraging my friendship with Jack. And especially that she was happy about the idea. Without another moment's hesitation, I replied.

I'd love to go! Can I get a lift with you?

Grinning happily at the thought of spending the day with everyone again, and in particular, with Jack, I waited patiently for her response. When she replied saying they'd be at my house at 10:30, I jumped out of bed and headed straight for the shower.

Although I hadn't even asked permission from my mom, I felt sure that she'd be okay with it. And when I joined her in the kitchen a short while later, I sat down at the benchtop and told her of our plans.

"You are so busy these days, Emmie. You're hardly ever at home anymore!"

With a shake of her head, she agreed that I could go as long as I stayed with my friends. Thankfully, she really liked the group I was hanging out with and was pleased to see me finally with friends of my own. The idea was still quite new to me as well and every day I remembered to appreciate how lucky I was to have met them all.

Thinking back briefly to my very first chance meeting with Millie soon after we'd moved to Carindale, I said a silent prayer of thanks. If she hadn't been so friendly and suggested that we hang out sometime, my life would be very different right now. That moment had been the start of my wonderful new life with a group of kids who I could genuinely call my best friends. It really was a dream come true.

Smiling at the thought, I sat at the kitchen bench and watched Mom making pancakes for our breakfast. I began telling her all about the party the evening before.

Starting from the moment I arrived, I talked about the amazing costumes the other kids were wearing as well as the cool games we'd played. She laughed about the limbo and asked how I had even managed to get under that limbo stick in Millie's pirate dress. That was when I mentioned Sara's costume and the fact that it was so much shorter than mine, but even so, Sara still managed to win the game.

Rolling my eyes at the memory, I shook my head with annoyance. And when Mom saw my reaction, she commented. "You don't really like Sara too much, do you, Emmie?"

My mother knew me too well. My look of disgust had made my feelings fairly obvious though. So it wasn't too hard for her to work that one out.

"She thinks she's the best at everything. She loves herself to death and tries to impress everyone. It's so annoying! And she's so two faced! I can't stand her!"

The words tumbled out one after the other. Like a raging storm of anger, I exploded in frustration. And did not have the power to stop.

Mom's eyes opened wide in surprise. She wasn't used to me talking about other kids like that. But then, before Carindale, I really never had too many kids in my life who I could talk about, let alone complain about. So I guessed it was new for both of us.

"Plus, she's evil!" I continued, angrily. "You should see what she's planning to do to Julia! Julia doesn't know, but I do. And it's so mean!"

I could not prevent the rant I was on. The mere mention of Sara's name had me in a state and the words flowed freely from my mouth. But as soon as I'd said them, I knew I had gone too far.

"You're not reading minds again, are you Emmie?" My mother's concerned expression was turning to one of irritation.

Frowning at me, she continued, "We've talked about this! I know it's hard but you have to stop! You can't be reading minds, Emmie. Especially with that strange man lurking about and knowing so much about you. Who knows what he's capable of! He could turn up at any time. So you have to be extra careful!"

Glancing down at the pancake that was going cold on the plate in front of me, I felt a small knot begin to form in my stomach.

The thought of that creepy man standing on our street corner, right by our house was too frightening. But I could not tell her about it. If I did, she'd have us packed up and moving again. My dream life would be over in a flash.

I stared silently back at her, not daring to tell her what I knew. It was something that I had to keep to myself at all costs.

"Emmie, please promise me that you'll try harder. I don't want you in danger! It's just not worth the risk!"

Nodding in agreement, I cut into the pancake on my plate and looked at her again before taking a bite.

"Alright!" I replied quietly. "I will. I promise."

Sometimes, however, promises are hard to keep. And although I had the best of intentions in mind and would never ever want to jeopardize my new life in Carindale, there was way too much going on and someone had to do something about it.

If only I had thought more about the consequences of my actions.

At the cinema...

As soon as we arrived at the cinema, we spotted Blake and Jack standing in the long queue lining up in front of the ticket counter. They were with a group of other kids from the party the night before. As we headed towards them, I held my gaze steady on Jack, who was chatting and laughing with the others.

Sneaking up behind them, Julia put her hands over Blake's eyes and said with a giggle, "Guess who?"

Grabbing hold of her hands, he twisted around to face her and then threw his arms around her in a welcoming hug. They were so cute together but I stood aside, feeling a little uncomfortable and not really knowing where to look.

Grinning shyly at Jack, I kind of shrugged, not sure what else to do. It was an awkward moment as we both stood there, Millie already deep in conversation with the other kids, and Julia and Blake completely engrossed in each other. For Julia and Blake, it was as though no one else existed.

Glancing again at Jack, I opened my mouth to speak, trying to think of something to say to break our awkward silence. I could tell he was also a little embarrassed, it certainly wasn't like him to be lost for words.

But we were unexpectedly interrupted by the sound of a familiar voice behind us. And we turned to find ourselves face to face with Sara and a couple of other girls who I recognized from the party.

I could feel my mouth open in surprise. The idea of Sara being there was just too much to comprehend. After complaining about her earlier that morning, she had turned up again to ruin our day. I tried to hide my frustration as I smiled at her in greeting.

"Hi, Sara. Wow! What are the chances of bumping into you here? Crazy!"

"I know! Such a coincidence!" she exclaimed happily, completely at ease with joining us. "This is supposed to be a great movie. We should all sit together!"

"What a good idea," I sighed, doing my best to keep my frustrations to myself.

Unfortunately for me though, I was the one at the end of the line, stuck by her side.

Forced to smile at each of her friends, in turn, I said hello but could not help myself noticing their downward glances as they took in the outfit I was wearing. I could see by their expressions that they weren't particularly impressed by my jeans and sneakers.

Even though they were my favorites and I was wearing a new top as well, my clothes obviously didn't match up to their standards. I wasn't even tempted to read their minds as I was quite sure their thoughts would not be ones I'd want to know. And it occurred to me that it was probably typical for Sara to have friends who judged everyone else by the clothes they wore.

That was when I noticed Sara's gorgeous skirt and top. Of course, there was no way I could compete with that. Her outfit was stunning and looked very expensive. She really did look super pretty, the pink midriff top was beautiful against her perfect skin and blond hair.

But then I realized I'd seen that top before and with a small gasp of surprise, I recalled it from the designer store in the mall. It had been hanging on the rack out the front and I was quite sure it was the one I'd seen her shove into her bag.

"Unbelievable!" I thought to myself. "She always looks so amazing. But half of her clothes are probably stolen."

With a shake of my head, I turned back towards the front of the line only to find that Jack had moved ahead alongside Blake. That left me at the end of our group next to Sara.

"*Great!*" I sighed. "*She really has ruined my day!*"

To make matters worse, when we all made our way inside the cinema, I noticed something else.

Somehow Sara had managed to grab a seat next to Blake. The tickets were numbered according to the seats we'd been allocated. So how had she done that?

I really had no idea what the answer to that question was but I could just imagine how Julia felt about having Sara on the other side of Blake.

Just as the lights dimmed, however, Jack who was the last to find a seat, sat down next to me and I looked up at him in surprise. I'd lost sight of him and wasn't sure where he had got to.

"Hey!" he said with his usual cheeky grin, "Do you want some popcorn?"

Offering me the carton, he kept his eyes on mine and I grinned happily back.

"Thanks!" I replied, feeling a warm glow inside. And immediately, all thoughts of Sara disappeared from my mind.

Taking a little popcorn, I settled back in my seat to watch the movie. The excitement I'd felt at seeing him in the line earlier had returned. And although I tried my best to concentrate on the storyline, with Jack sitting so closely at my side, that was difficult to manage.

I was aware of him at my side through until the very end of the film. His laughter was infectious and I found myself constantly cracking up. And when his hand brushed mine as the two of us reached for popcorn at the same time, the electric bolt that hit my fingers was just the way I imagined a lightning strike would feel. Except, in this case, it was the best feeling ever!

The feeling...

After the movie, we all headed to the mall for something to eat. There was a huge group of us and in the crowded food court, it was difficult for everyone to find a seat. But Jack and I had both raced to an empty table and managed to find enough chairs for our small group so that Millie, Julia, and Blake could all sit down alongside us.

We'd also managed to lose Sara and her friends in the crowd. At least, there was no sign of her right then and we guessed that either they couldn't find a spot to sit or had decided to eat somewhere else.

Glad to be rid of her, we munched hungrily on our burgers, while at the same time laughing loudly about the film. We hadn't expected it to be quite so funny but we were still cracking up over how hilarious it had been.

Mid-laughter, however, I caught sight of someone I knew it was best to avoid and quickly glanced back down at my plate. I was hoping desperately that he hadn't caught my eye and that he had no idea we were all sitting nearby. Then when I dared to look up once more, he had disappeared.

Breathing a sigh of relief, I kept my thoughts to myself and focused once more on the chatter of my friends. That was until I felt a weird and uncomfortable sensation at the base of my neck. I tried to ignore the familiar prickle but it was quickly becoming more and more noticeable. It was the same old feeling I always got when something was terribly wrong. Instantly, I knew that somewhere amongst the crowd, there was a pair of unwanted eyes staring threateningly towards us.

Glancing around, I looked into the crowds of people, most of whom were all chatting and eating and focused on each other. No-one was taking any notice of us. We were just a group of kids sitting at a table minding our own business. Why should we be of interest to anyone else?

Normally that would be the case in a crowded shopping mall. Everyone going about their day, doing what they needed to do, or just hanging out with friends. That was all we had wanted when we left home that morning; to see a movie together and hang out and have fun. There were lots of other random kids as well as all the ones from the party the night before, sitting at nearby tables, doing exactly the same thing as us.

Everyone, it seemed, was oblivious to our small group as we sat there together.

Everyone that was, except him.

Dilemma...

Should I tell the others? Should I alert them to the danger in our midst?

I knew he was trouble. His thoughts carried across the mall to my own, loud and clear. I'd become quite good at focusing on one set of thoughts alone. That was a skill I'd developed over the years. Before that, my head was a mix of crazy chatter from everyone around me.

But right then, all I could hear were his thoughts and his alone. Even the voices of my friends sitting alongside me had become muffled; almost like a dull background drone of sounds that blended quietly together.

It was the actual words being spoken in his head, the ones that I was listening to that bothered me the most.

I'd finally spotted him in the crowd. But I was quite sure he didn't know that I had. He thought he was hidden amongst the surrounding people. They were all focused on a demonstration for some type of new toy that had just been released. Kids and parents alike seemed fascinated by the new invention.

Ryan was pretending to concentrate on it as well. But really, he was watching us.

Watching and plotting.

Plotting and planning his revenge.

But he had to be stopped. I could not let him hurt my

friends. They had done nothing wrong. Wasn't it my duty to protect them?

My dad said in his letter to me that I had a gift and that I should use it to help others. Well, this was my chance.

Breaking out of my bubble of concentration, I shook my head from the daze that I was immersed in. And that's when I heard the voices of my friends.

"Emmie?"

"Emmie, are you okay?"

"Emmie, what's wrong?"

Staring from one to the other, I looked at their confused and worried expressions. Millie, Julia, Blake, and Jack. Each of one of them was staring at me with concern.

"Emmie?" Millie repeated, grabbing hold of my arm and giving it a firm shake.

Gulping down a breath of air, I noticed the beads of perspiration that had formed on my cheeks and felt the flush of heat on my skin. Gradually, I felt the fog in my head disappearing.

"I'm okay," I mumbled quietly, unsure how to explain what had just happened.

"It's like you were completely zoned out!" Millie exclaimed. "You had your eyes open but it was as though you weren't there."

"I thought you must be having some sort of seizure or

something," Julia added, a worried expression on her face. "Are you sure you're alright?"

"Yes, yes, I'm fine," I smiled weakly, trying to reassure them all. "But I might just go to the bathroom. I'll be back in a few minutes."

I stood and quickly walked away, ignoring their protests and the girls' offers to come with me. There was something I had to do and I needed to do it quickly. It was my chance to prevent something terrible.

Shaking my head with dismay, I tried desperately to focus. That zoned out state had never happened to me before. It was something completely new, something I had never experienced. But in those moments, I was sure that my mind reading power had been stronger than ever.

I also saw it as a sign, a sign to do something. Anything to prevent the disaster that was on its way.

Spotting him amongst the crowd, I headed towards him. Walking in his direction, I made sure not to lose sight of the person I knew I had to confront. The crowd had thinned a little and he'd become clearly visible amongst them. And then he caught my eye. He stood, staring at me for a moment, that intense, blood tingling stare of his connecting with my own fearful gaze.

Turning quickly, he stomped off in the opposite direction.

Hurrying after him, I quickened my pace. I could not let him get away.

Just as I had shortened the distance between us and almost

caught up to him, he glanced back. And dodging abruptly around a large group of kids milling in the center of the walkway, he broke into a run.

Then, within seconds, he had disappeared from sight.

I continued at a run but I knew I had no hope of finding him. The mall was overflowing with holiday shoppers, families and kids of all ages, and Ryan was nowhere to be seen.

But I knew he was there, somewhere amongst the crowd, hidden away once more.

As I stood there, helplessly scanning the faces of the people in the crowd, reality took hold.

What would I do if I were able to catch him? What *could* I

do?

My original plan was to confront him, to tell him I knew exactly what he was up to and that he had to stop or...

Or what?

I'd call security? Or I'd call the police?

As if they'd believe me anyway.

And what then? Tell them that I'm a mind reader and cause all my mom's fears to really come about?

They'd either lock me away in some type of asylum for the insane or fill me with medication so that I'd never be the same again.

Or, worse still, they'd believe me and I'd be kidnapped.

It would be like signing a death warrant.

Signing my life away, the way Mom had always feared if anyone ever found out what I was actually capable of.

"They'll lock you away forever!" she had said to me, over and over.

"You'll become some type of scientific experiment and they will never let you go. They'll want to do tests on you and keep you a prisoner until they find out your secrets. They'll be desperate to discover what makes you capable of doing what you do. That will be the end of us, Emmie. I will never see you again!"

Deep down, I knew she was right. I'd always known it.

And I was afraid.

Brushing the tears of frustration from the corners of my eyes,
I turned around and headed back towards my friends.

The Vision...

The following days passed by quietly. And for that I was grateful. I'd certainly had enough excitement for one week and was keen to avoid being out in public for a little while. I was on edge and found it difficult to relax. Nothing I did was of any help.

I tried listening to music, watching movies on television, distracting myself on the computer. I even went to a yoga class with my mom, but that had little impact. At my mom's insistence, I'd tried yoga a couple of times before. She always found it relaxing so I thought I'd give it another go. The teacher kept reminding everyone to just breathe and relax. I could see that she did it easily.

I tried as hard as I could to copy the teacher's poses and take deep breaths, but I was hopeless. Perhaps I was just too uptight for it to have the effect that it should.

Although I'd learned that in yoga, to get the proper benefits, you really need to switch off all the thoughts racing around in your head, and put away the negative emotions. But for me, there was so much going on that I was really struggling to do that.

And then on our way home, I spotted him again.

"OMG! What is going on?" The thoughts raced through my mind as I caught his evil gaze through the car window.

The strange, black-coated man was back. Standing on the corner, watching and waiting.

But what on Earth did he want and why was he here?

Between him and Ryan, the pressure and worry were becoming too much and I could feel myself beginning to unravel.

When my mom pulled into our driveway and we made our way to the front door, I glanced anxiously back. It was just a slight turn of my head, nothing noticeable, but I could see him watching.

He was definitely there this time. It was not my imagination running wild, it was not a vision that I'd conjured up in my panicked state. He really was there! And I knew his eyes were directed towards me and watching. Watching and waiting once more.

Rushing up the front steps and into the house, I locked the door behind me. Mom had headed for the kitchen to begin preparing dinner. We were having tacos, usually one of my favorite meals, but right then I had no appetite whatsoever.

I moved towards the window frame and stood at the side, glancing out the crack between the curtain and the window. I had a clear view down the street and could see the cloaked figure still standing there, as still and straight as a perfect statue. The only thing moving was his cloak which blew slightly in the breeze.

I was fairly certain that I could not be seen from my spot and decided to take advantage.

It was something that had just come to mind.

Emmie Ferguson, you are a mind reader! So do what you do best and read his mind!

I have no idea where the thought had come from, although I had a sneaking suspicion, it might have been my dad. He was not always with me, but when he did appear, it was as though he whispered silent thoughts in my ear. That was the only explanation I could think of. It was either that or intuition telling me what to do. But I preferred to think of it as my dad.

Focusing intently, I stared towards the mysterious figure. His cloak continued to blow in the gentle wind and he remained firmly in his place, just like a sentinel on red alert. But I was also alert, and rather than being the victim, for a change I decided to take control.

What was the man thinking? What was going on in his head? Surely his thoughts right then revolved around me. And that was something I was determined to find out!

Taking a deep breath, I concentrated like I had never concentrated before. And all of a sudden, I could feel myself slipping away, to another place, another world.

In my head out of nowhere, appeared a vision. It was a clear picture and it played out in full just like a movie on TV. I could see a room full of people sitting around a long conference type table. But I felt fairly certain they weren't your average everyday type of people. I also felt certain that they were like me. Amongst them was one young child but the rest were adults and I had a distinct feeling that they were all mind readers.

And then, quite abruptly the vision in his head changed. The room full of people disappeared and instead, I was staring at my own face. Even in my dazed state, I could feel my stomach churning and a tight knot taking hold.

This was very different to anything I'd ever experienced before. Usually, I just heard the thoughts of others. I knew exactly what they were saying in their minds but out of the blue, I was seeing images as well; the exact images that were floating around in his head.

Then the words came too.

I have to get her. I promised them I would.

But not yet. The timing's not right.

Soon.

It'll be the right time soon.

"Emmie? Emmie, I'm calling you! Can you please come and help me in the kitchen. I've called you three times already!"

My mother's loud voice broke through the fog in my head and with a gasp, I glanced around me. Taking a deep breath, I turned back to the window again. But he was nowhere to be seen.

From where I stood, the street was deserted. Deserted and silent, with the flicker of street lamps bringing a glow to the blackness of night that had just begun to shroud the street in darkness.

Moving quickly away but still overcome by what had just taken place, I headed towards the kitchen.

The last thing I wanted was for Mom to find me standing there and begin asking questions.

That was definitely the last thing I needed.

The surprise guest...

The next morning, I woke to find the house deserted. Roaming from room to room there was no sign of my mother anywhere. It was not like her to leave without warning and I felt a small tremor of concern bubbling inside me. But then I spotted a hastily written note left on the kitchen benchtop...

Gone to the market. Didn't want to wake you. Be back soon.
Mom xxx

In my groggy and dazed state, I remembered vaguely that it was Wednesday, the day that Mom usually took a trip to the farmers' market to pick up our weekly supply of fresh fruit and vegetables. Then, glancing at the clock on the wall, I realized how late it was. I'd slept much later than usual. It had taken me quite a long time to fall asleep the night before so it was probably quite late by the time I had finally drifted off.

Visions of the creepy man had remained in my head and I'd been unable to shake them. At one point, I had almost gone to my mom's room to ask if I could hop into her bed. But eventually, I must have fallen asleep.

I was still feeling uneasy and this was made worse by the fact that I'd been left in the house alone. Usually, that wasn't a problem for me at all but after what I'd witnessed the evening before, I was on edge.

Tentatively, I made my way to the living room and my viewing spot at the window's edge. The blinds were still drawn closed and I quickly peeked out onto the street. Much to my relief, there was no sign of him. Apart from a couple of kids riding their bikes along the pavement, the street was deserted and there was no one else out there.

Just as I turned to head back to the kitchen for some breakfast, I heard the sound of my mother's car in our driveway and was relieved to realize that she must have returned already. Moving towards the front door, I pulled on the handle and opened the door wide. But rather than the familiar sight of our little blue sedan, I was faced with a large yellow 4-wheel drive vehicle that I had never seen before.

Who on earth can this be?

The thought rushed through my mind as I squinted in an effort to see who was behind the tinted glass of the windshield. But the glare from the bright light of the morning sun made it difficult for me to make out who was inside the car.

A mysterious figure opened the passenger door and stepped onto the grassy verge alongside the driveway. Then, with a wave in the passenger's direction, the driver reversed onto the street.

When the figure walking up the driveway towards me was no longer silhouetted by the sun's beams behind him, I gasped with realization.

OMG! It's Jack!

And I'm gawking like an idiot while I stand here in my pajamas! This is so embarrassing!!

I could feel my face flush red. I hadn't recognized the car and I certainly had not been expecting a visit from Jack. It was so typical that of all mornings, I'd chosen that one to oversleep and hadn't even got dressed yet.

Running my fingers quickly through my hair in a desperate attempt to smooth out the fuzzy mess, I watched him walk towards me, the smile beaming on his handsome face.

"H...Hello!" I stammered, "What are you doing here?"

"Aww, nice to see you too!" he laughed.

Shaking my head in apology, I stumbled on my words once more. "I...I didn't mean it like that. It's just that I...I wasn't expecting you!"

Normally, I'd be thrilled that Jack had decided to visit, even if it was unplanned. But the fact that I was standing there in my oldest PJ's, which were an over-sized pair from years gone by that still happened to fit me, was too embarrassing for words. The singlet top and shorts were a matching set, bright pink and covered in an assortment of rainbow colored elephants. They'd been my favorites for so long and when my mom first bought them, they were all I wanted to wear.

Standing there and facing the boy I had a huge crush on only a few feet away, I was not at all comfortable being dressed in eight-year-old pajamas.

Staring at me in confusion, he took a quick glance at what I was wearing, and then it was his turn to explain. "Sorry, I'm a bit early. Dad dropped me off on his way to work. He was starting late and offered to give me a lift."

Still trying to work out the reason for his visit, for a moment I stood in awkward silence. That was until he mumbled hopefully, "The girls should be here soon, shouldn't they?"

Like a light bulb abruptly switching on in my muddled brain, I finally realized what had happened.

"Jack," I replied with a shake of my head, "The girls have gone to the city with Millie's mom today. We've all planned to hang out tomorrow. Remember?"

"What?" he stared at me, his face showing total surprise, obviously struggling to comprehend what I was saying. "No way! You've got to be kidding me? But I'm sure your text said Wednesday!"

Lowering the skateboard he was holding, he reached into his back pocket for his phone and scrolled through his messages. I stood watching as he searched for the group message we'd sent each other a couple of days earlier.

"I can't believe I did this!" he shook his head as he read the words in clear view on the screen in front of him.

I could see his embarrassment as he shook his head in self-disgust. "I'm such an idiot! I was sure it was planned for today!"

Laughing, I tried to make him more at ease. It was clear that he was feeling pretty silly and looked ready to turn around and leave.

But the truth of the matter was, even though I'd been caught dressed like an eight-year-old, I was secretly pleased that he was there. And when I invited him to come inside, I watched the grin return to his face.

Then in typical Jack style, he made a comment that had us both laughing. "Nice outfit by the way!"

Feeling the flush of red on my cheeks, I gave him a playful shove on the shoulder, before heading through the open front door with him following along behind me.

"I'm going to get changed!" I grinned, directing him towards the living room. "I'll be back in a minute." And as I raced to my bedroom, I vowed to get rid of the elephant pajamas once and for all.

With an excited flutter deep in my stomach that I seemed unable to shake, I rummaged through my cupboard in search of something pretty to wear. Deciding on a pair of white shorts and a sky blue top with a swirly silver sequinned pattern across the front, I quickly got dressed before rushing to the bathroom to brush my teeth. As I ran a comb through my tangled and messy hair, I thought again of how I must've looked when Jack saw me standing at the front door.

Trying to forget that image, I glanced at the reflection staring back at me from the large mirror. I was hoping to make a good impression on Jack, especially after the way I'd looked only moments earlier, and with the excited flutter working its way through my entire body, I headed back out to the living room.

The sight of his beaming smile immediately pushed all anxious and embarrassed thoughts from my mind. And when he eagerly accepted my offer of something to eat, his smile growing even wider at the mention of food, we made our way into the kitchen in search of some breakfast.

It was such an unanticipated turn of events and I had certainly not expected to be sitting at the kitchen bench alongside Jack that morning. But as we munched on our cereal, I had no idea whatsoever of what the day would bring or the secrets that would be shared.

And as it turned out, the most important secret of all was the one that surprisingly came to the fore.

The question...

When my mom returned about an hour later, a large bag of fresh fruit and vegetables as well as other supplies in her arms, she was surprised to find Jack sitting alongside me at the kitchen bench.

She laughed at the number of cereal bowls and plates topped with toast crumbs scattered across the bench top. It looked as though a whole family had just finished breakfast and it was obvious that a lot of food had just been devoured. Jack had not eaten breakfast before leaving home and it was clear to both Mom and me how much that boy could eat.

It had taken two huge bowls of cereal, one that he particularly liked as he'd never tried it before, and 4 slices of toast with an assortment of toppings, to finally fill him up.

Amazingly enough, he still had room for one of the freshly baked muffins that Mom had brought home with her.

During the time we'd been sitting there, Jack and I had talked non-stop and the time had passed quickly. That always seemed to be the case whenever we were together. There were no uncomfortable silences, (at least, not when I was caught in my oldest pajamas), and there were never any boring moments either.

Instead, the kitchen was filled with constant laughter and I felt more relaxed at that moment than I had all week long. Not even my mom's yoga class had had the calming effect that a visit from Jack created. He was like a dose of much-needed medicine...perfect for the soul.

I was quite sure that he felt the same close bond with me. While I also suspected he may also "like" me, the way I "liked" him, I was determined not to invade his privacy by checking in on the thoughts going through his head. I respected him too much to do that and if he ever found out I was reading his mind, I was sure it would be the end of our friendship. And that was something I definitely wanted to avoid.

After my mom unpacked all the bags of fresh fruit and vegetables, she went to her office to get caught up on some overdue work. And so Jack and I continued talking. Up until then, all we'd talked about was the upcoming Carindale's Got Talent competition, which was only two weeks away, and what we'd both been up to since last seeing each other at Hayden's birthday party.

But then Jack mentioned that he'd spotted Ryan in the mall the day before, and I felt an instant chill of apprehension work its way down my spine. When he went on to describe the strange scenario during his visit to the local phone store, the chill in my spine turned to one of fear.

Apparently, Jack's dad was interested in buying a new iPhone and had promised to give Jack his old one. However, his dad had been talking about this for ages and it still hadn't happened. So, to speed everything up, Jack had decided to visit the phone store himself in order to do the necessary research that would convince his dad to finally go ahead. This, of course, would lead to Jack getting his dad's old iPhone at last. And even though it was an older model, it was still in perfect condition and a thousand times better than the one he currently owned.

Jack's phone was a relic from the past; an old hand-me down from his mom that constantly needed recharging as it was always going flat. And to make matters even worse, it had a cracked screen that was so bad, the messages could barely be read, which I guessed was probably the reason he'd misread our group text. Obviously, Jack was in need of a new phone as soon as possible and could hardly wait to be given his dad's.

So that was what led him to be browsing through the phone store that was situated dead center in the middle of the mall. This would not have even been worth mentioning except for the fact that he happened to notice Ryan Hodges had also entered the store. He was checking the phones on display in the row next to where Jack was standing.

At first, Jack had taken little notice. Ryan was weird and had caused so much trouble at school that he wanted as little to do with him as possible. So he pretended not to see him. But when Jack caught Ryan staring towards him, he moved to another section of the store.
Within seconds, however, Ryan appeared in the same aisle

and continued staring. From the corner of his eye, Jack could see Ryan's gaze remaining focused on him.

"I stared back," Jack explained, "but he didn't flinch. So I asked him what he wanted, and he didn't say a word. He just stood there and death stared me. It was so creepy that I ended up having to leave the store just to get away from him."

"But the freaky thing is," Jack continued, "I had this really strong feeling that he was following me. It was so weird. I don't know what his problem is!"

That was when I blurted my response. I was unable to hold my thoughts back any longer, and the words poured out in a rush.

"Jack, I'm really worried about Ryan! He keeps turning up and I'm sure he's planning to do something bad!"

I stared in silence at Jack's stunned reaction. I could see he was surprised at what I'd said. But at the same time, I could tell that he also suspected something was going on, and it wasn't good.

At one stage, I'd thought Jack might actually have mind reading abilities. I wanted so badly for this to be true that I'd tried to test if it was really the case. And when that didn't work, I attempted to teach him to read minds the way I could. This didn't work either so I'd given up.

But I was still fairly sure that even though he couldn't read minds, he was able to pick up on other people's thoughts and what they were feeling. I decided that this must be intuition. It was the only explanation I could think of. It was something that I was familiar with and related it to the prickly sensation I sometimes felt at the base of my neck; the one that instantly told me something was wrong. It was like a sixth sense that I had.

I was convinced that Jack had that sixth sense too. He was able to pick up on things going on around him, the way that I could. And although his ability stopped there, he definitely had what I liked to think of as 'good intuition'.

I was certain that was the reason we got on so well. I could connect with him in a way I had never connected with anyone else before. Not even Millie. Even though Jack and I hadn't known each other very long, it was as though we understood each other; so much so, maybe we were simply meant to be together.

While that was probably just wishful thinking on my part and something I wanted to believe, I wondered if it might really be true. The whole concept was so romantic that my stomach fluttered at the thought.

In that split second, I made a sudden decision. And without taking another moment to consider whether I was doing the right thing, I popped the question that I thought I would never ever ask.

"Jack, if I tell you a secret. Do you swear on your life that you will not tell a living soul?"

The words came out in a rush. In fact, it was almost a garbled mix of gibberish and at first, I thought he had no idea what I'd just said. But then comprehension dawned in his expression and I knew that he had understood every word.

However, I did not expect his reaction. I'd just asked him the most important question of my life and he responded by laughing! Well, I guess it was more of a chuckle than a laugh but whatever it was, it was definitely not a laughing matter. Not as far as I was concerned!

"Jack, this is serious! If I'm going to tell you this, you have to promise! It's our secret and ours alone. Nobody and I mean NOBODY can ever know!"

His smile disappeared. Whipped away in a flash, a look of serious curiosity took its place. With my eyes focused seriously on his, I did not even flinch. Without blinking, I held his gaze for what seemed an eternity. Although in reality, it was probably only a second. But it felt like forever.

I knew I could trust Jack. I didn't feel the slightest doubt at all which was why I had asked the question in the first place. It was a secret that could not only affect my future, it could ruin everything. But I had no choice. I had to tell someone. It was either that, or I was I would fall apart.

Before continuing though, I had to hear the words from him. I needed him to say those two words.

"I promise!"

Just as he opened his mouth to speak, my mom walked back into the kitchen.

Almost caught out...

I stared at her in silence. I could feel the guilt wash over me and I hung my head, unwilling to look her in the eye. If I looked at her she would know. Of that I was sure. And that would be the end of everything. We'd be packed up and moved out of Carindale before the week had ended. There would be no more hanging out with the best group of friends I'd ever known. I would completely miss their performances at Carindale's Got Talent and I would never see Jack or Millie again.

My stomach churned in turmoil and a feeling of nausea took hold. Should I wait for Mom to leave and continue with my plan? Should I go ahead and share my inner most secret with the boy who had become my closest friend? Or was my mother's sudden appearance in the kitchen right then, a sign? A sign that I was doing the wrong thing!

"Am I interrupting something?" she asked with a laugh. "You guys are awfully quiet all of a sudden!"

Mom looked from me to Jack and back again, her gaze lingering on my face. I glanced up at her apologetically, trying to prevent the flush of guilt that was creeping slowly up my neck.

Needing to get away as quickly as possible, I jumped up from my seat. "Wow! Is that the time already?"

Staring up at the clock with a pretense of disbelief, I continued, "It's such a beautiful day outside, Jack. We shouldn't waste any more time indoors. Let's go and do something!"

Realizing it was time for a quick exit, Jack quickly got to his feet and started gathering together the dishes that were still laying in an untidily on the bench top. Quickly helping him, I grabbed the pile and carried it to the sink, with a promise to wash them all up later.

"Is it okay if I go with Jack down to the skate park? He brought his skateboard and I can just ride my bike there?" I looked at my mom, waiting impatiently for her to answer.

A small frown was obvious on her face but she nodded her head in agreement. "Yeah sure, that's fine. You're right, it is a beautiful day outside, and it would be a shame to waste it!"

She looked curiously at both of us in turn and I knew she suspected something was going on. I could see the curiosity in her expression and felt sure she'd ask me about it later.

I would just have to make something up. But right then I was desperate to get out of the house and away from her prying eyes. So I headed quickly for the garage to get my bike.

Clipping up the buckle of my helmet, I glanced at Jack who was right behind me, skateboard in his hand. I didn't say a word to him, but I could see he understood. We didn't need to speak to communicate the thoughts racing through each of our heads. Both of us seemed to be able to work out what the other was thinking. And I read Jack's thoughts without invading his mind. There was no mind reading required.

Our spoken words would have to wait until we were safely out of earshot of my mother. As well as super-sonic hearing, she had the same sixth sense as I had, and I was not at all willing to risk being heard.

Jack, who clearly understood my apprehension, waited for me to get organized. He then skated along behind me as I pedaled in the direction of the skate park. It was situated towards the very end of my street, about a mile down the road, but I was glad for the chance to think.

Realizing what a miracle it was that my mom had not overheard our conversation in the kitchen, I said a prayer of thanks. It was something I always did when I felt I was being looked after. Her appearance had not been coincidental though. I was sure of that. Either it was a warning to keep quiet or a warning that she was within earshot. It had been a stupid idea to share my secret while she was in the house.

Choosing to believe the second alternative, I pedaled even harder. I was desperate to get to the skate park quickly so we could sit down and talk.

Since making up my mind there was no turning back.

The secret...

As soon as we found an isolated seat in a quiet section of the park where no one was around to bother us, Jack focused on my face. He was looking at me curiously and waiting for me to speak. I could see that he would not pressure me to begin, but instead, would allow me to start in my own time and when I was ready.

"I promise!"

Two simple words...they'd been exactly what I needed to hear. And now that they'd been spoken, I was struggling to come to terms with what was going to come next. The moment felt surreal. I seemed to be watching myself from afar. Looking on and witnessing the very point in time where I made the biggest decision of my life.

I was about to share something that had been a part of me for as long as I could remember. Sworn to secrecy by my mom, I'd vowed to always keep that secret intact. But sometimes promises just had to be broken.

Julia and Blake were my friends and if anything happened to them, I'd never forgive myself. Ryan had made it his mission to harm them.

I could choose to keep that piece of information to myself, then sit back and allow the danger to unfold. Or, I could ask for help. To me, the second choice was the only one I could live by.

Both my parents had told me that I should use my gift to help others. But I couldn't do it on my own. Telling Jack was the only way.

There was also the issue of the mystery man in the long black cloak to deal with. I knew that he was an important piece of the puzzle. But for now, that problem would have to wait. My friends had to come first. Before it was too late.

I looked at Jack as he waited patiently by my side, staring at me with those beautiful brown eyes fixed intently on my own. Then, taking a deep breath in an effort to find the courage I needed, I spoke the words I never thought I'd hear myself say.

"I'm a mind reader!"

He stared blankly back at me, waiting for more. His lips twitched as a smile threatened at the corners of his mouth. Although he knew it was not a time for jokes, he was struggling not to laugh. Raising his eyebrows, he continued to stare, his expression a mixture of laughter and curiosity.

"Really!" I stated firmly and with a serious nod of my head. "I can read minds!"

A frown formed on his brow while at the same time, he chuckled with amusement. "Okay."

It was a single word response. It had two syllables but it spoke volumes.

My own frown deepened as I stared back at him. I knew he could see I was not impressed.

"This is not a joke, Jack! I can actually read minds. Like…for real!"

"Okay!" he repeated again, this time nodding his head instead of shaking it.

His expression had turned serious and I was sure it was his intuition kicking in. He could sense this was not a time for humor or for joking around and he didn't dare make fun of me. But at the same time, he was struggling to comprehend what on earth I was talking about.

Then came the logical response, the one that I'd been expecting. "If you can read minds, then what am I thinking now?"

"You're thinking that I've lost my mind, that I've gone crazy. Either that or I'm playing some kind of trick on you!"

"Yeah," he replied, "that pretty much sums it up." He was grinning now and clearly not convinced. Turning around, he began to search in every direction.

"Don't worry," I replied, "Blake and Julia aren't going to jump out of the bushes. No one is going to suddenly appear with a video camera and get you on film. You're not going to be the brunt of some joke that ends up on Facebook or Instagram for the whole world to see."

He laughed again, raising his eyebrows once more. "It's pretty obvious that's what I was thinking, Emmie. Anyone could have told me that! If you can really read minds, you've gotta prove it! What number am I thinking of right now?"

"42," I replied without hesitation.

His grin widened. "Lucky guess!"

"It wasn't a guess, Jack," This time, I couldn't help my own grin. "Ask me another question."

"What color am I thinking of?"

"Red!" I responded immediately. "Come on Jack, that's way too easy. You can come up with something harder than that!"

I laughed again, my confidence growing. This was becoming fun. I had never had the opportunity to openly prove myself before. Usually, it was the opposite, where I was blocking people's thoughts, trying to prevent them. Being asked to focus on a person's mind with their absolute approval and share what I found, was something very different.

Taking a moment to consider what I'd just said, he grinned once more and nodded his head, his brain kicking into action. *I don't know what she's up to. But this one will catch her out. There's no way she'll know the answer to this!*

"What did I do when I left the mall yesterday?"
Focusing intently, I read the thoughts swirling through his mind, and the visions suddenly appeared. Just like a movie playing through from start to finish but on fast forward, I recounted the events that he was picturing in his head.

"You went to Blake's house to rehearse for the competition. The girls weren't there, just you and Blake. But before you started you shared some left-over pizza that Blake found in the fridge. It was pepperoni and you had two slices."

I watched the smile on his face falter as I continued.

"Then you went into the garage to rehearse your song for the competition. Blake was working on his drumming solo and you wanted to practice your rap. You asked for his dad's opinion. You think it could be better somehow and you want to improve it."

Jack stared at me, his mouth wide open. He didn't say a

word. But after a moment, he glanced around him again. He was expecting Blake to suddenly appear, rolling around with laughter at the idea that Jack had believed my story.

"Blake's not here, Jack," I explained, as I smiled at him gently. "I know this is really hard for you to understand, but I really can read minds."

He jumped to his feet then and shook his head in firm denial. "Nah, there's something going on! You've spoken to Blake, haven't you? He told you all that stuff. That's the only way you could know!"

"It was your idea to ask me what you did yesterday, Jack. How could I have known beforehand that you'd even ask me that question?" I stared intently at him but he was still refusing to believe.
"Alright," I added, "ask me something else."

"Okay." A determined look had appeared on his face. "What did I do for my 8th birthday?"

"Wow! That's a random question," I grinned. "But yeah, no problem. I can tell you all that. I just need you to focus on that day in your head. Remember what you did and I'll tell you exactly what you're thinking about!"

He looked doubtfully at me, but sat tentatively down and closed his eyes.

Then, without even having to think about it, the words poured from my mouth. "You were very excited! It was your first really big birthday party and you were allowed to invite all your friends from school. You had it at a place called 'The Big Boing.' It's full of huge trampolines that you can bounce on and has pits with chunks of foam to jump into. It's located downtown and you've been back there with Blake a few times since."

He opened his eyes and stared at me, his expression turning to one of awe.

"Keep concentrating," I prompted. "Close your eyes again and think about that day."

His brow creased into a frown but he didn't say a word. When he closed his eyes, I continued.

"There was a kid there called Zac. He went flying down one of the slides and crashed into a little girl. He nearly knocked her out and her mom complained. Both of you got into trouble."

I was becoming excited then as the whirlwind of thoughts raced through my own, and the words poured out in quick succession.

"Blake was there too and he gave you the coolest present. It was a really big super soaker water pistol. You couldn't wait to try it out. As soon as you got home, you started firing water at everyone. Your mom threatened to take it off you!"

Jack's eyes flew open, his mouth wide opened and his expression one of stunned disbelief.

Jumping to his feet again, he stammered the words, "That...that's not possible! You weren't even there! Seriously, that's just freaky! How could you know all that stuff?"

Right then his head was spinning. His thoughts and feelings were filtering through to my own in a vivid rush of colors and sensations. A mixture of awe, disbelief, shock and last of all, fear, came rushing through my senses. It was all too much for him to comprehend.

"So you really can read minds?"

Sitting triumphantly alongside him, I grinned with pride. Finally, he believed me!

"Are you like, some type of government spy or something? Are you here on some sort of top secret mission?"

Now it was my turn to laugh. "Jack! You've been watching too many movies! Of course, I'm not a government spy! I'm just a regular kid."

"Aaah, I don't think so!"
He was still shaking his head and still trying to understand what was going on. It was all too much for him and I could see that I needed to explain.

"Jack, seriously, I'm normal in every other way. It's just that for some reason, I can read minds. I don't know how it happened or why but I've always been able to do it."

"My dad was a mind reader too!" I added, hoping this would add some credibility to my story.

Jack's fear was gradually fading away and in its place was an intense curiosity to find out more. He was struggling to come to terms with it all and desperate to put all the pieces of the puzzle into place. It was clear to me that I needed to start from the beginning.

But I was more than happy to do that. Finally, I'd been able to share the one personal detail that I'd kept secret for so long and I was overwhelmed with intense relief. The hardest part was over. And the rest was easy.

So I began. I recalled every detail, starting from my childhood and the very first moment I realized I knew what my parents were thinking. I recounted it all. And the entire time, Jack barely moved a muscle. His eyes did not stray once from my own as he took in every single word. The time passed by but both he and I were absorbed in the tale being told. I was the speaker. He was the listener. And his expression was one of utter fascination.

"Wow!" I'd finally finished speaking and his eyes were wide as he sat stock still, trying to process the incredible story I had just shared. "That is incredible!"

Staring into space, he did not budge. Apart from shaking his head for about the hundredth time in the past hour, he remained perfectly still alongside me.
And then I remembered the most important detail of all. "Jack you can't tell *ANYONE!*" I emphasized the last word before continuing. "You *have* to keep your promise. *This is our secret and no one else can know!*"

He looked solemnly towards me and nodded his head in agreement. And then came the words I so desperately needed to hear. The reassurance that would erase the tiny feeling of doubt that was taking hold in my gut.

"Don't worry, Emmie. I promise! It's our secret."

As if to reassure me further, he reached for my hand.

And then he gave it a gentle squeeze.

It was that gesture that meant more to me than anything.

Unease...

I have no idea how much time passed by but we continued to sit in that same spot, comfortable in the silence that surrounded us. By then the park was deserted, everyone had probably gone home for lunch. But still my hand was in Jack's. It was as though nothing else existed and it was a moment I wanted to last forever.

Now that I'd shared my secret we seemed more connected than ever before. And I knew that he felt it too. It was like a magnetic pull and even though I'd blocked his thoughts from entering my own, once again, I knew exactly what he was thinking.

That was one of the first things he asked me when he finally opened his mouth to speak. "Are you reading my mind now, Emmie?" A slight frown of concern had appeared on his face and I could see that the idea bothered him.

"No, Jack," I responded, giving his hand another squeeze. "I wouldn't do that. I promise. If you want me to know something, then you can tell me yourself."

I'd already explained how I had stopped listening in on people's private conversations, the ones that went on inside their heads. First of all, because it got me into too much trouble, but most importantly because it wasn't the right thing to do; especially to my friends.

I knew that he believed and trusted me. Just as I believed and trusted him. We'd been drawn together for a reason. I could see that now. But that trust could not be broken. It was too precious.

The one thing I hadn't mentioned...was the mystery man in the black cloak. For now, I just wanted to focus on one problem at a time. The mystery man could wait.

I'd seemed to have developed an inner-confidence and strength. And I knew that this had come from the support of the person sitting alongside me. With his belief and faith, I felt that I could manage anything. At last, my mind reading skills really did feel like a gift. Because like all gifts, it should be shared and used to help others. I sensed my dad's presence nearby and I was convinced that he would approve. He had more than likely sent Jack my way, to give me the help I needed.

"So, what's going on with Ryan Hodges?" It was Jack who brought up the question. It was the whole reason I'd decided to confide in him in the first place, but still so caught up in the moment, I hadn't yet mentioned that important detail.

"You said back at your place that Blake and Julia are in trouble? What's going on, Emmie?" Jack turned to me then, a serious expression on his face.

He'd obviously been thinking everything through; all of the events that had come to pass, and was now as concerned as me at the thought of Ryan's strange behavior.

I went on to explain everything I knew. Right from the first time I'd become aware of the strange kid in the mall, who had been so intensely focused on Julia and her friends. Back then, I'd only met Millie. I'd heard so much about the others though and I remembered myself staring in fascination at each of them. When Ryan's thoughts filtered through to my own, I knew instantly that something was very wrong. He wanted revenge. And was obsessed with Julia and Blake getting what he believed they deserved.

It was creepy. But more than that, it was scary. And once again, I was glad to have someone to share my fears with.

"We have to do something, Jack. But I have no idea what!"

"Yeah," he agreed. "That kid really freaked me out yesterday. I can tell that he's got serious issues. Who knows what he's capable of?"

"But all we can do for now is be on red alert," he continued. "And maybe warn Blake, Julia and even Millie, to watch out for him as well."

"Okay," I replied, with a nod of my head. But Jack's words did little to ease the sense of foreboding that was working its way through my senses.

And at the feel of the familiar prickle at the base of my neck, I glanced quickly around. But all I could see was a row of leafy green foliage rustling gently in the afternoon breeze.

"It's getting late, Jack. We should head back home. And besides, I'm starving! I bet you are too!"

With a grin in his direction, I tried to ease the tension I was feeling, but it did little to help. And hopping onto my bike, I followed behind Jack. He pushed along on his skateboard avoiding the rutted sections of the pavement as we headed in the direction of my house.

Understanding...

That night when I went to bed, I knew that I'd be lying awake for hours on end. But this time, it was with a huge smile that I pulled back the covers and snuggled beneath the quilt.

Rather than the panicked feeling of worry and anxious tossing and turning, I was quite happy to remain awake, staring out the window at the glowing moon hovering so peacefully in the darkened sky beyond. It was a night perfect for star gazing and dreaming. A night made for wishes to come true.

Right through to the inner most part of me I knew. I knew that I'd been heard; that my hopes and prayers had finally been answered.

Yes, I now had a wonderful group of friends.

Yes, I'd connected with the boy I'd been secretly admiring for what seemed like forever.

But most importantly of all, I'd shared my secret with someone who understood. Sure, I had my mom. But she didn't fully comprehend what I went through every day. I knew she cared about me and would do anything she could to protect me. But when it came to understanding my world and the effect my unique ability had on my existence, she had very little idea.

Telling Jack, and knowing I had his trust and support as well as his promise to help me in any way he could, was like a tightly padlocked box full of top secret information had been opened and shared.

It also felt as though an incredible weight had been lifted from my shoulders.

Before confiding in him, there was the expectation from my mother that I must not tell a living soul of what I was capable of. And at the same time, I'd been given the responsibility of using my power to help others.

I wanted to do that. I wanted to keep quiet and protect us both. I wanted to do everything I could for people who needed me. I really did. But it was so much harder than it sounded and I simply did not know how it could be done.

"You've been given this gift for a reason," Mom always reminded me. "You must put it to use, Emmie. And use it wisely!"

But what did that even mean? If I had to remain quiet, how could I use my mind reading abilities? How was I supposed to help others when I was sworn to so much secrecy?

The more I thought about it, the more I was sure that I'd done the right thing.

After arriving back from the skate park and eating the toasted sandwiches Mom prepared for us before she went out, Jack and I moved to the living room and found a comfortable spot on the sofa. And that was where we remained until my mother returned three hours later. During that time, Jack and I talked and chatted, and spoke some more.

He wanted to know everything about my ability. He was fascinated and eager to learn all that he could. What meant the most to me though was the fact that he was not interested just for the sake of playing tricks on people, or breaking rules or doing things that might get me into trouble. He didn't suggest anything like that. But the question he eventually asked, showed me how much he really did care.

"How does it feel, Emmie?" his face was a mixture of curiosity and genuine concern as he spoke those words. "I mean, how do you cope with being the only one, the only one with this power but forced to keep it completely to yourself?"

He was thinking of the impact it all had on me. And that meant more than anything. Then I felt the gentle squeeze of his hand, the reassurance he really was there for me; that was the best thing ever.

As I lay in bed, thinking over the events of the day, the wide smile remained in place on my face. I was feeling more secure than I ever had before.

Even my fear of the cloaked man had subsided. I'd nudged it away, to the very rear of my mind. And as far as Ryan was concerned, I was certain that with Jack's help, we'd manage to devise a plan, a plan that would rid us of his torment once and for all.

They were the thoughts floating through my head as I finally drifted off into a deep and comforting sleep. I could still feel the touch of Jack's hand in mine and I was sure there were also still remnants of the smile on my face when I woke the next morning.

But if only I hadn't become so carefree. If only, I'd taken into account how far Ryan might actually be willing to go, to seek the revenge he was intent on. Perhaps then I would have been more prepared and better able to help prevent the terrible disaster waiting to happen.

If only I'd known.

If only...

Unexpected...

I couldn't believe my luck. It was the day that all of us had planned to hang out together which meant I'd get to spend the day with Jack. Again.

Everyone arrived at my house soon after ten o'clock. And this time, I made sure to be dressed and ready. No more elephant pajamas! The night before, I'd thrown them into the laundry basket to be washed. I'd also given my mom strict instructions to add them to the growing pile of donations for the charity store downtown. I was sure that some little girl would probably love a pair of pre-loved pajamas covered in rainbow colored elephants. And after my embarrassment the day before, I was happy to see them go.

After everyone had arrived and we'd devoured the entire batch of chocolate chip cookies that Mom had baked for us, we headed off on our bikes to visit Blake's dad's new music studio. There were very few people in the area who catered for kids interested in private music lessons. Most had to travel long distances to learn guitar, drums or keyboard as well as for singing lessons, and these were what Mr. Jansen specialized in. So as soon as the studio had become available for lease, he decided it was time to get moving on his idea.

He'd spent several days doing some minor renovations and was planning to begin lessons the following week. In the meantime, Blake had asked if the band could use the studio to rehearse. Blake said that his dad was reluctant at first but as he was planning to be there working anyway and would be available to supervise, it was a good time for us all to go and check it out.

Using the studio for band rehearsal had two huge advantages. First of all, it was filled with a heap of professional equipment, much more professional than what was in Blake's garage. Added to that was the fact that the studio, which was already quite well soundproofed, was located on the edge of an industrial area with only a few houses nearby.

According to Blake, this was the main reason his dad had agreed for the band to use it; anything to avoid the continued complaints from neighbors who lived on their street. Because the band had been practicing so often lately, everyone was tired of the noise. This was something I was not surprised about, as I'd heard first-hand how loud the band could be.

To me, the day felt like an adventure. Being able to cycle to the studio with the others was exciting in itself. As we rode along the bike path at the side of the road, I considered for about the millionth time how lucky I was to be a part of this wonderful group of friends. It was definitely shaping up to be a summer to remember.

At one stage, Millie, who was cycling alongside me interrupted our conversation to ask me a question, one that I had not been expecting. "So, Emmie, what's going on with you and Jack?"

Although I was thankful that the others were out of earshot, especially Jack, I was unable to help the grin that instantly appeared at the corners of my mouth. Then, shrugging my shoulders in denial, I replied with a shake of my head, "What are you talking about, Millie? There's nothing going on!"

By then she was laughing and demanding an answer. "Oh,

come on, Emmie! I'm not blind. I can see the way he looks at you!"

"What? What do you mean?" I could feel my face flush a deep shade of red.

"Emmie, he can't take his eyes off you! Has he asked you to go out with him yet?"

"What??? No! Of course not, Millie. We're just friends!" I was laughing at her words but deep down inside, I was thrilled at the idea. And the fact that Millie was encouraging it, was better still.

"If he hasn't yet, I'm sure he will soon!" she exclaimed with a firm nod.

And with that, she pedaled a little harder, moving in front of me to avoid a slight ditch in the path just up ahead. But she couldn't resist a quick glance and a cheeky grin as she passed me by.

With a sigh of happiness, I continued to cycle along behind her. The day seemed full of magic and I wondered if it could possibly become any better. A warm glow filtered through my senses and I knew it was not from the rays of sunshine that were beaming down from above.

In my dreamy state, I almost missed a sharp turn in the road and came close to colliding with the raised cement edging of the curb. Slowing down a little, I continued to pedal but soon realized I'd begun to fall behind the others who had disappeared around a corner. I then had to pedal a little harder to catch up to them.

When I turned the bend, I caught sight of them further down

the street. The area was sparse at first with a few solitary houses and some vacant blocks.

But I could make out a row of buildings towards the end, one of which I assumed must be the music studio.

The level bike path that we'd been cycling along had come to an end, and the street was rutted with potholes. So I had to slow right down to avoid the ditches in the bitumen. Taking in the untidy state of the houses as I cycled past, I took note of one, in particular, that was overgrown with long grass and thick shrubs.

I have no idea why I stared all of a sudden into the front yard of the ramshackle property that looked neglected and uncared for. Perhaps it was the slight movement that caught my eye or the flash of color that I noticed which urged me to look in that direction. But when I did, it was not the unkempt state of the house or the flash of blue clothing. Rather, it was the face of the individual who stared back that seemed to make its mark and cause me to gasp in surprise.

In that moment, I felt the warm glow inside me abruptly turn cold. And even though it was a hot summer's day and a bright sun was beating its vivid rays of glorious sunshine onto the earth below, I felt the goose bumps rise up on my flesh as they prickled and danced on my skin.

Later on, when I thought back to that moment...I remembered his surprised expression and was still not sure who was more shocked right then. Him or me?

And I also wonder if the events that followed would have been avoided if I had not looked in his direction, or if I had kept pace with my friends and passed the house before he stepped out the front door and onto the pavement.

But then I guess I will never know because that is not what happened.

I recognized him instantly and after realizing who I was, his expression turned to one of anger and then hate. I could feel it radiating from his thoughts and it almost knocked me from my seat as I pedaled frantically by, desperate to escape his presence as quickly as possible.

But as I made my way down the street, desperate to reach the safety of my friends, I could feel his gaze burning into my back. And without daring to look behind me, I knew beyond doubt that his eyes were following me, every foot of the way.

Rehearsal...

When I caught up to the others, they'd already reached the studio door and were being greeted by Blake's dad. I risked a quick glance back and could still see the lone figure standing at the end of the street looking in our direction. His blue t-shirt stood out, but from where I stood, I could not make out his face. But I knew it was him and I opened my mouth to warn my friends.

Before I had a chance to speak, Mr. Jansen began to welcome us all inside, ready to show off his new studio to the keen young musicians. He loved the fact that Blake and his friends had formed a band and were entering a competition. He was willing to encourage them in any way he could. Already, he'd suggested that I also take up an instrument so I could join in the fun. And it was something that I was seriously considering.

Right then, however, learning an instrument was the last thing on my mind. My senses itched with an uncomfortable feeling that I was struggling to contain. But the excitement that was bubbling amongst everyone else as they took in the professional area around them, was impossible to ignore. Blake had burst forth in an unstoppable flow of admiration for his dad and what he was creating. And I wasn't quite sure whether it was Blake or his dad who was more proud.

After having spent many hours there already, helping with renovations and set-up, Blake was completely familiar with every detail. As we followed him up the staircase and from room to room he explained what was involved in all the high-tech sound equipment. There was a very cool brand new drum kit and a heap of other instruments available as well.

It was all very impressive and everyone was interested in seeing the full set-up.

And then I heard Jack's voice above all the rest, "Mr. Jansen, this is awesome! I can't wait to hear how we sound!"

That was what prompted everyone to begin getting themselves organized. They were impatient to get started, and I could not bring myself to spoil the moment. It was just not the right time to announce the fact that Ryan Hodges appeared to live in a ramshackle house at the end of that very street.

I was still coming to terms with that idea myself and there would be no gain in sharing that unwanted piece of information right then. So I convinced myself to remain quiet for the moment and allow all thoughts of Ryan to disappear from my mind; for the time being at least.

Disaster...

It wasn't until a couple of hours later, that we all realized how late it had become. Everyone was so engrossed in the music that the morning had passed quickly by. As promised by Blake's dad, the sound quality was better than ever and even though I was biased, I thought the band was amazing. They had certainly improved since I'd last heard them perform, so obviously, all their practice had been worthwhile. Mr. Jansen was also very impressed and that was what mattered most. When he assured them that they were definitely ready for the competition, they all beamed with delight.

Although Millie and Jack both wanted to continue practicing for their solo acts, Jack's complaints of hunger reminded everyone else how hungry they were as well. That was when Blake's dad offered to drive down to the pizza store located just a few miles away to pick up some pizzas for lunch.

At first, he suggested that Blake go with him to help carry all the drinks and the several boxes of pizza that he planned to order. But when I realized that Blake preferred to keep rehearsing and make the most of his time in the studio, I offered to go instead.

When his dad tried to call the store to do a phone order, the line was busy, so we decided to head down there and order over the counter. It was all such a good plan. The guys could keep practicing while Mr. Jansen and I left to get the food.

When we arrived though, we found a very flustered young girl behind the service desk who was trying to help package a particularly large takeaway order. At the same time, another customer was waiting impatiently to be served. So we ended up being forced to wait nearly forty minutes for our own order to be ready.

With the back seat of the car filled with boxes of pizza and sodas, we headed down the busy road back to the studio. But as soon as we turned the corner into the quiet street that led to our destination, both of us knew instantly that something was terribly wrong.

I think we each spotted the plumes of black smoke rising into the sky at the same time. And almost in unison, both of us exhaled loud gasps of shock.

The fear seeping through me was like a suffocating blanket. It seemed to begin at my fingertips and work its way quickly through my senses until it reached every part of me. It was so overwhelming that I struggled to breathe.

Blake's dad, slamming on the brakes and pulling to a sharp stop in the middle of the road, shoved open the car door and jumped out, running...

Engulfed in waves of hysteria that were washing over me in driving torrents, I threw open my own door and followed him.

Staring in shock and horror at the sight in front of me, I stood frozen to the spot as flames leaped into the air.

And with a thundering crash, the brand new multicolored sign that displayed the words MUSIC STUDIO, fell in a broken heap onto the ground; while at the same time, the fire raged behind it.

Racing towards the burning inferno, I was alerted to the

loud screaming noise in my ears. Then, in an abrupt flash of recognition, I realized suddenly that the hysterical sound was coming from me. It was my own voice calling the names of my friends, who I knew must be trapped inside.

Whether it was instinct or intuition, I had no idea. But deep within the depths of my soul, I was certain that Ryan Hodges was to blame.

***

Find out what happens next in

Mind Reader – Part Two: Books 4, 5 & 6

You can choose to buy each book individually or purchase the set at a DISCOUNTED PRICE!

***

Thank you for reading my book.

If you liked it, could you please leave a review?

Thanks so much!

Katrina x

Follow me on Instagram

@juliajonesdiary

@katrinakahler

And please LIKE Julia Jones' Facebook page to be kept up to date with all the latest books in the Julia Jones' series…

https://www.facebook.com/JuliaJonesDiary

Have you read the Julia Jones' Diary series yet?

Book 1 – My Worst Day Ever

is available now.

If you'd like to read the series, you can buy the collection as a combined set at a DISCOUNTED PRICE...

Julia Jones Diary

Books 1 – 5

Available on Amazon and all large online book retailers...

Many of the following books can also be purchased individually or as a combined set so that you can read the entire collection at a DISCOUNTED PRICE!
Just search for the titles on Amazon or your favorite online book retailer to see what is available...

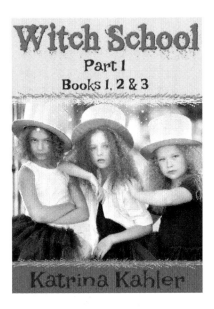

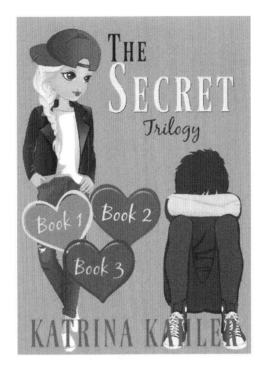

18809283R00171

Made in the USA
Lexington, KY
23 November 2018